Chapter

"Whew! Boy, ain't it cold!" The old man slapped his gloved hands against his thighs. He shook his head letting drops of snow fall on the polished plank floor. "Mr. Beull, I'd appreciate it if you would shake your head outside the building, please! We have enough problems keepin' the children from creatin' a mess, much less you, Sir"

Eustice Beull watched as the Headmistress gathered her skirts and glided down the hallway. He grinned at her passing, well aware of what the kids said about this formidable woman. "Miss Shay's feet don't never touch the ground. That's why she can walk like that. All quiet and silent, sneakin' about. That's why she always wears them long, long skirts! Why, that woman may not even be blessed with feet a'tall!" A chuckle started low in Eustice's throat as he stooped his old back and wiped at the pool of snow beginning to puddle under his boots. Yeah, Miss Shay was a force to reckon with but in his dealin's she was a fair and educated woman; someone Eustice admired.

Eustice Beull had been the handyman and custodian here at the Lawnwood School since it had opened in 1925. He ran his cold fingers proudly over the beautifully appointed Oklahoma stonework. He strolled to the arched front door dodging this child or the next rushin' to get into the building, to get warm.

Eustice watched as the snow silently skittered through the schoolyard and caught mercilessly in the wrought iron fence. He squinted his eyes against the glaring brilliance and the rising sun. "Funny kinda snowfall", he said to himself, "Feels just a little unnatural." "Mr. Beull!" Eustice spun on his heel as his name rang out through the silent hallways.

"Now I know wool- gatherin' is an important event around these parts but we have a school full of children and it's colder'n a witch's teat in here! Excuse my language, Mr. Beull but my nose is about to freeze and fall directly from my face to the floor. Do you think you could do a little somethin' to save me, Sir?"

Eustice glanced at the scrawny, good natured man sidled up beside him. He held a handkerchief to his face and had a shawl draped over his stooped shoulders. Eustice never understood how such a young fella could look so pale and unhealthy, especially here in Oklahoma. But, here he was, big as life sneezin' and hootin' and shiverin' to beat the band.

Mr. Dover came from somewhere North where Eustice envisioned everyone to look this way, a little unhealthy, and frankly a little bit bug-like. Oh, the women seemed to find him attractive but he'd do nothin' in the cotton field, that's for certain. "I'm sorry Stanley," Eustice took a step back from the coughin' man. "I just got a little caught up in watchin' the snow is all. I'll get to crankin' on that stove directly."   "It is lovely, isn't it Eustice?" said the smaller man. He wiped his nose on his handkerchief and laid a friendly hand on Eustice's shoulder. "I've seen snowfall up to the second story windows where I came from, but this is different. Soft and sneaky."

The man turned a soft brown eye toward the old man. "This is better somehow, cleaner." "I reckon," said Eustice. "I ain't never been past the Hughes County line, Stanley, so I wouldn't pretend to know better. I'd best get to that stove 'fore Miss Shay slides back out here ta give me hell!" The men shared a nod of the head and a fast, knowing grin as they parted ways leaving the snow to fall and pile where it would.

Eustice Beull made his way to the big, chrome plated stove that served as furnace to the entire stone structure. The school was big as far as country standards go. Four big classrooms divided down the middle by a long hallway. Each room was blessed with tall casement windows and chalkboards covering two walls of each room. The ceilings were tall and elegant. Crisscrossed with heavy wooden beams and flue-work passed into each room driving warm air in and down from the ceilings.

Children traveled from all over the county to attend this handsome school. The teaching staff was top rate and the sports teams were nothing to be scoffed at. Lawnwood School had always made a name for itself around these parts.

Eustice stopped to check the coal bin before he entered the furnace room. He noted the bin would have to be filled before the week was out, especially if this cold weather held up. He always tried hard to keep things in tip top shape and keeping the coal bin filled was an important task in his eyes. 'Those children couldn't learn if they was cold!' he always said.

Eustice always puffed his chest with pride just a little, as he strolled past the glass case that held the trophies. The children had done well through the years and earned enough trophies to prove it. Eustice had known every child whose name was engraved on those Loving Cups. He had attended every game and every Spelling Bee.

He'd watched the first crop of kids grow and have children of their own. The names were always familiar in a small community like this, just the faces changed. Eustice lightly touched the glass as he passed by the case that held those shiny Loving Cups and statues of sports figures. So many kids had grown up under his watchful eyes.

Eustice stoked the stove with the skill of a man made for the task. His gloves steamed in the new born heat. When he was finished he hung the coal shovel on the wall next to the stove and slowly wandered back out toward the front of the building. "Well," he thought to himself, "maybe

I ought be thinkin' about doin' a little shovelin' 'fore those kids let out for recess. Miss Shay'd have my head iffin' any windows got broke out due to snowballs!" On his way out the door, shovel in hand, he dropped a note on Miss Shay's desk reminding her to order the coal.

Arlie Booker never liked Social Studies. He knew when he got a bit older he'd be joinin' his Daddy at the peanut mill and would never give one miller's damn to the War 'a 1812 again. He sat at the back of the class lettin' Mr. Dover drone on and on in a steady stream of words and places Arlie liked to use to ease himself into a soft twilight sleep. He sat in the warm classroom with his head tipped toward the ceiling, mouth open, almost droolin' as his eyes grew heavier and heavier. He listened to the snap and crackle and somewhere in the back of his brain he heard the clicks and clanks of ole' man Buell stokin' the stove. Arlie's head fell back and was cradled by the uncomfortable wooden back of his desk. Through his hooded eyes he watched a pink cast form on the flue pipes heating the room to a narcotic warmth.

Arlie shuffled his long legs that barely fit under the desk anymore. "Next year I ain't comin' back to this school." he thought to himself. "Next year I'm gonna work the peanut crop!" He watched the persistent pink travel the length of the stovepipe and make the curve up thru the ceiling. His eyes grew heavy and his mouth fell open. A little snore escaped waking him once again. Tiny whispers of smoke started playing gently along the stovepipe. Arlie watch in fascination as the tiny white whisper turned a soft felt gray. "FIRE!" he yelled!

Chapter 2

No one would ever forget the day the school burned. In a small town these things pass for generations handed down like precious keepsakes. The stories get twisted and heroes become villains. Villains become saviors as the stories shift and change to suit the tellers.

"File out! File out! No need to push! You are going to be just fine! Go line up along the berm by the pond...go on now! Stay with your teachers! You need to stay orderly…your mothers and fathers will be along to collect you soon."

Miss Shay glided quickly among the children, touching heads and counting. "Stay out of the blowing embers! Just be very careful where you stand. Try to stay in a nice straight line so I can get everyone counted."

Most farmers resented sending their children to school in the first place. They needed the hands to work the peanuts or hay. But this new school made a difference. The government said education was the wave of the future and everybody wanted the best for the kids. So off they trudged. Bagged lunches in hands. Clean overalls and greased down hair to learn "Readin', Writin' and 'Rithmatic".

They were to learn things that their parents knew little of. A hard day's work and a handshake was the way these folk did business. Things were changing though, and along with the trouble in Europe, people were getting nervous. They knew education was becoming a necessary thing, even farmers needed a little schoolin' in these troubled times.

This big, handsome school had changed the lives in this county in subtle ways. Kids that had never had contact with folks other than their own families or on Sundays at church were tossed together for the first time. Teachers from out of state were hired to educate.

No one had sent their children out with the intention of watching the schoolhouse burn on that cold, cold day in January.

The little ones stomped their feet and spun in place to keep warm. They caught snowflakes on their tongues and stood huddled together or found a sister or brother to cling to. Teenage girls held hands and chatted quietly, hugging younger brothers and sisters or keeping an eye out for boyfriends. They stood on the berm watching the snow fall from the gray sky in an endless stream. It was all so quiet and pretty....'til the fire roared up and scorched their faces with its fury. 'Till the roof of the schoolhouse fell with a terrible roar, scattering sparks and ash on the new blanket of cold whiteness.

Miss Shay glided from group to group counting and touching each head as she traveled. She muttered to herself trying hard to keep track.

From time to time she would turn and watch the fire spreading along the roof-line of her beloved schoolhouse. Suddenly a look of confusion crossed Miss Shay's face. "Wh-where's Becky Warner?" she stammered, almost to herself...then louder, "Where's Becky Warner?" Finally, in an act of desperation...she shouted, "Where's Becky Warner?"

Chapter Three

Becky Warner jumped down the stairs of her family's old farmhouse. She danced her way to the kitchen pecking her mother on the cheek as she swung by, grabbing a piece of toast and sip of fresh milk. "Why you in such a good mood on this dreary, snowy day, girl?" her mama asked, a soft smile came and went on her powdery lips. Becky was a handful it was true, but she just couldn't help but be tickled by her pretty daughter. Everybody was. The girl shined like a new penny and Deloris Warner knew it. She expected great things in the life of her teenage girl. She knew most parents wanted that but Becky was different. "Mama, every day is a good day! It don't matter how much fluff tumbles from the sky!" Becky leaned over and kissed the top of her little brother's head. "You feel like makin' a snowman today, little boy?" She asked, buffin' her brother's unruly blonde hair. "Nope...but I'd like to go to the picture show come Saturday! Please! Please take me Becky!" Becky winked and grinned at the pleading boy. "Gotta see what Saturday brings now don't we Sonny?"

The tinkly sound of girl's laughter made its way from the hall doorway. "Oh my! I gotta git! The girls are here already!" Becky pulled a heavy coat from the hall hook and tied a scarf around her blonde curls. She stepped out in the quiet snow to meet her friends and make their way to the schoolhouse. No one knew then that Becky would never be seen by her family again.

"My goodness it's damp out here today ain't it?" Connie Buckman snugged down into her heavy coat as the girls walked. Becky Warner stuck out her tongue and caught a few snowflakes as they fell, "I like it!" she said, kicking the snow ahead of her. "Oh, you like everything! Ain't no big deal for you to like sumthin'." chuckled her buddy. "Now that ain't true. I'm not all that fond a this little podunk hole in the pasture we call a town! I just cain't wait to step my foot outta here and git on to Memphis or Fort Smith, maybe even Chicago or New York!" Becky skipped a few steps and threw her hands in the chilly air. "Just imagine...I won't be beatin' foot to git anywhere anymore and none a this ugly homespun either! No more sewin' up my own dresses if I want somethin' new. I'll just drop in at some big department store somewhere and buy what I want! I'll be ridin' in a fancy car and sportin' silks and satins. Yep, that's exactly the life I have planned!"

Becky took a quick playful spin in the snow and turned her bright blue eyes to her friends. "And y'all know I'm gonna make that happen doncha now?" Becky gloated.

The girls laughed and dreamed their way down the road and through the heavy wrought iron gates of Lawnwood School. "Hey, hold up a sec!" Becky chimed as she scurried around the corner of the beautiful brick structure. "Come on girls, let's visit the outhouse before we go in the door!" "Becky it's cold! I jis wanna git in the warm school!" Edna Bolls complained. "Come on now! Won't take but a second!" No one could deny Becky when she was on a mission. The three girls made their way to the spacious facilities built just behind the school. They were just outhouses but still they were kept clean and bright. The "girl's room" had a nice big mirror and pails of water for the girls to 'freshen up' in.

"Here Edna, hold this purse for me will ya?" asked Becky as she entered the room. As they all watched Becky rolled the waistband of her skirt a good three inches from its original resting place. Then she fluffed her hair and applied a coat of lipstick to her pouty lips. They all watched as Becky transformed from a simple farm girl to a movie star before their very eyes. "Where'd you git that color lipstick? Ain't never seen the likes a that over't the Miller Drug!" said Edna. "Well no, silly! My Aunt Phyllis sent me this all the way from Nashville! Nashville, Tennessee that is!" Becky rolled the sleeve of her coat down to reveal a half pack of cigarettes.

She pulled one from the crumpled pack and lit it, letting it drip from her painted lips. "Oh Lord Sister, you gonna git us all in some deep water with all this fuss!" Connie shook her head and reached for the cigarette. After a fast drag she swished her hand around the room to disperse the smoke. "We gotta go girls! Old lady Shay's gonna be glidin' on out here any second!" Connie stuck her head around the corner. Becky laughed. "You just worry way too much Connie Buckman! Bein' the reverend's child is the worse thing coulda ever happened to you, I swear!"

The three fifteen year olds rounded the corner of the outhouse and sped into the warm, comfortable schoolhouse to join in for another day of being teenagers.

Chapter Four

Casey heard the door slam seconds before the assault. Benj rolled in like a freight train derailed... "Get up, Casey!" She shouted, bangin' on the door. "Oh hell no!" Casey replied, tuggin' the old quilt up around her neck.

Benj dropped to the bed and lightly moved Casey's blonde hair away from her ear, "You're gonna like it!" she whispered softly. Casey opened one eye and gave Benj the stink eye. "Why are you wakin' me on a Sunday morning at..." she lifted her head and glanced at the clock on the bedstand.

"7:03! Jesus Christ, Benj you know damn well this is my only day to sleep! Get out a here! Why are you home anyway? Why aren't you out working?" Benj rolled over on her back knocking Casey half out of the bed. "I am working. I just came home 'cause I found something you're gonna love and I wanted to show it to you. Now if you could just humor me for a half hour I promise you...guarantee you...you're gonna love it! You're up anyway." Casey flashed the stink eye once again but she knew if Benj was going through all this trouble it had to be good. She swung her legs over the side of the bed and sleepily headed for the bathroom. "This better be damn good." She mumbled, stumblin' around the corner and rubbin' her eyes.

"See, this is why I worry so much about this little car of mine Casey! I told you, it's rough as a moonscape out here in the boonies." Benj slowly navigated her tiny car through mud and potholes big enough to swallow a truck much less her car. Casey rolled her eyes and announced "We live in the boonies. This is just slightly more boonified." Benj gripped the wheel hard. "Yeah, but this car is made for city drivin' and not much more." She gritted her teeth as another divot took it's toll.

Benj spent her early mornings delivering newspapers to the rural areas around her town. It wasn't something she wanted to spend her life doing but it kept the bills from stacking up and adventure seemed to follow her everywhere.

Benj had discovered wonder after wonder in the untold miles she skated morning after morning. She was always up before the sun rose and the fur started flyin'. It was a quiet and peaceful job Benj did at her own pace. A lovely reprieve from driving a delivery truck through wild Chicago traffic.

"Wow! This is crazy cool out here huh? Funny how the landscape can be so different in just a matter of miles." Casey stared out the window of the little car. Her farm was located on land that had been cleared for years and farmed for most of it. What she was seeing now was raw and virginal. If it had been cleared at one time nature had slithered back in and reclaimed what had once been stripped of her. "Do people actually live out here Benj?" Casey asked in amazement. "Well, somebody reads those papers I deliver! Or paper their bird cages, or make paper pirate hats outta them. Yeah, people live out here; kinda different huh?" "I'll say!"

muttered Casey. "I've heard this land all belonged to some oil company back in the day. They had some sort of town out here where you could only buy from the company store, you know...like Pullman in the Old Chicago days, and we all know what good came of all that!" Benj started singing in a low voice..."I owe my soul to the company store...."

"Holy Shit!" Casey grabbed the edge of the dashboard and dug in for dear life. "What the hell is that?" Casey glanced at Benj and stared back out at the beautiful ruins in front of her. "Benj, what is this place? What happened here?" Casey couldn't take her eyes from the artfully placed

Native stone structure before her. The elegant, glass-less windows curved in perfect telling tales of a much more glorious time. "What is it Benj? Is it a school, a meeting house? No, it's a school all right.

Why would there be a schoolhouse way out here? And man, what a beauty of a schoolhouse it is!" Casey dangled her head out window of the car taking in every nook and cranny she could see from her vantage point. "Come on Benj! Let's go in! Let's explore! Wow, this place is fantastic!" Benj laughed and grabbed Casey's shoulder as she started to open the car door. "You're gonna have to go callous your fingertips Googlin' this place first, Case.

I've gotta drop you off and get myself back to work. I knew you'd love it. I'll toss a little more gas on the fire for you though. The cornerstone says 'Lawnwood School 1925', now there's a good place for you to start." With that, Benj backed the car out and started for home. Casey spun around as far as her seat-belt would let her. "Whew! That's somethin' Benj!" Casey breathed. "Was it worth the rude awakening on a Sunday morning?" Benj asked, already knowing the answer. "Now you have all day to work your magic, Casey.

You can Google yourself into a stupor while I finish my route." She glanced at Casey. Yeah, she knew that look. Casey was already spinning stories and wiling her way in and out of those old stone arches. Yep, Casey was already lost in a mystery and that was all it took. Benj smiled to herself.

Chapter Five

The snow fell softly and the fire raged. The children of Lawnwood School stood on the berm and watched as the flames grew and over took everything they knew as familiar in the schoolhouse. They shivered as their faces ran with sweat from the conflagration. As the sun dipped, the fire seemed to take on a life of it's own.

The stories varied with every telling. The flames were high, the wind blew like a hurricane through the fire feeding and coaxing it, bringing to life a terrible destruction.

"Oh, I saw Mr. Buell run back in the schoolhouse after we was all safe on the berm.

He was a-hollerin' Becky's name and we could see him searchin'. He was tippin' tables and runnin' through like the dickens. Then he was gone."

"Mr. Buell come out with the rest a us, then we heard him screamin' for Becky. You could see his outline through the winda."

"I heard him shoutin' out. Then his voice sounded scratchy and soft...but you could still hear him, then not."

"Mr. Buell looked like an angel through that burnin' winda. You could see him black against the red

and yallow a the fire. He was yellin'
and lookin' ever where for Becky.
Then the smoke just kinda wrapped
around him and he was gone! I think
Jesus done come took him to
heaven...right when we was watchin'."

Local School Fire

Lawnwood School burned
yesterday as a result of a
malfunctioning coal stove. This tragic
fire resulted in one death and one
student missing. The deceased man is
Eustice Buell, 64, the longtime
custodian and caretaker for the
school. Missing is Rebecca Warner,
15, a student attending Lawnwood

School. Any information about Miss Warner would be greatly appreciated.

"Come on, Mr. Dunbar, let's get you in your chair." Casey steadied the elderly gentleman and carefully helped him into his old recliner. "There you go. Let me get you started on a treatment while I get your breakfast going. Bacon and French toast sound good today?" "That sounds good, Honey. I could go for somethin' sweet this mornin'. I sure do miss my coffee though. Nothin' stirs that hankerin' for a good cup a coffee like a dose a maple syrup." He shook his head. "Don't reckon I'll ever see another cup a that delight again." Casey smiled at him and patted his spotted hand. "Ah, you're doin' terrific Mr D., spry as a kid at ninety-five! You could out work me if you wanted, I know it!" Casey ducked around the corner and rummaged in the 'fridge for the breakfast makings.

"Hey Mr. Dunbar? You know anything about Lawnwood School?" She asked, dropping a couple slices of bacon in a wrought iron skillet.

"What's at?" the old man started from a quick snooze. "Lawnwood School you say? No, no I don't reckon I recall that place at'all." Casey dropped a piece of white bread in the egg batter and let it soak.

"At that place out past Greasy Creek? Big stone school, burned?" He asked. Casey peeked around at the gentleman. His head was down and he almost looked ready to drift off again. "I didn't know it burned but yeah, that's the one. You remember it now?" Casey asked. "I remember playin' basketball out there, nice gym...pretty girls." A slight smile crossed the corners of his mouth lifting 10 years along with it. "Back then the girls would bake pies and cookies and take 'em to the games.

That was a nice tradition. Us boys lived here in town thought we was somethin'. Town Boys. Those folks out there, we called 'em "country". We was a little stuck on ourselves then I fear." The man chuckled as the memories flooded back. "They had a good team back then, boy, I'll tell ya, Honey. Oh, those girls was sweet and pretty from out that way. I was a skinny boy with curly hair, and I got offered some cookies that's for certain!"

His smile shined bright as he thought about those days. Casey swore ten years dropped from his face. Then he grew quiet and his chin dropped to his chest. "Becky Warner." he said and dropped into a shallow sleep.

Chapter 6

"Hey Benj! You wanna go out and poke around a little bit at that ole' school today?" Casey asked hopefully.

"No, I'm tired. This heat is kinda gettin' the best of me; may be allergies. I think I'm gonna spend some time curled up in my bed today." Benj rubbed her forehead and tried to sneeze. "I think I'm gettin' behind on my rest." Benj flopped over on the sofa and folded her arms around herself.

"You're not gonna fall asleep on the sofa fully dressed are you?" Casey gave Benj the stink eye and tapped her with a sneaker. "You're not gonna lay there and sleep like a hillbilly are you? That's not your bed." Benj rolled over and opened one eye. "What?" She almost yelled. "Not everybody is as crazy as you are about making their bed every day and having perfect sheets, Casey...leave me alone!" Two cats jumped on Benj's hip and started purring and kneading, finding the perfect spot to settle in for the long haul. Casey watched as Benj's head slowly sunk into the sofa pillow and a low snore started rumbling from her. "Benj!" Casey said softly, "How do I get there?"

Benj flopped over on her belly. Casey knew once she was asleep it would take an act of Congress to wake her up again. "Highway 7...red roof....turn right...follow the road." Casey quietly slipped out the front door, locking it behind her. She knew Benj would sleep for hours. The afternoon was hers to enjoy.

Casey slowly pulled up to the ruins of the old schoolhouse. The air was still as a tomb and hotterin' Hades. When Casey was a child she remembered warm Illinois days. Standing in the yard listening to the birds and the soft breezes. She always felt like she was the only person alive on those wonderful afternoons. It was often like that here in Oklahoma, only hotter, much hotter. Casey stepped from her truck and immediately felt sweat start to bead around her hairline. Casey had long, thick hair, and while it was a nice head a hair it was rough on these sultry days.

Casey swept her hand along the broken wrought iron fence. The gate hung catty-whompus on one elderly hinge. The sidewalk behind the fence was buckled and battered. Casey closed her eyes and let the tiny fingertips of thousands of children seep into her thoughts. She plopped herself on the top step leading to the magnificent archway that stood untouched and unsullied in deep yellow stone. Casey held tight to the gate as she imagined kids running and playing...grabbin' this gate and swingin' their way in the schoolyard. A smile crept it's way over Casey's upturned face. She could feel it, she could smell it. Coal smoke and chalkboards. Two kids pounding their detention out with erasers against the building . Slamming the long cowhide covered blocks together and cleaning the dust from the previous day's learning, their punishment satisfied. A flagpole in the yard, three boys in short pants carefully and reverently attaching the flag and hoisting it aloft.

Casey opened her eyes. For a second she sat confused. This often happened. She was disappointed to be snapped back to her own time. She flicked out her foot and kicked a loose stone down the sidewalk. She slowly stood and glanced around, exhaling heavily. Casey pushed her sweaty hair off her face and let the breeze cool her. She turned slightly and stooped to pick up another stone. This one came from a pile in the middle of the yard. As she kicked again she saw the remains of a pole, a flagpole long gone. "Damn!" She said aloud. "Somebody wants me to know somethin'!"

Casey was surprised to see the sun was starting to sink and the breeze had picked up considerably. She turned and looked up at the stone arches like they were an old friend. "Guess I drifted off on ya there, huh?" She asked, a slight smile touching her lips. She put her hand to her forehead shielding her eyes. "You know I'll be back."

Chapter 7

"What did you do fun this weekend Miss Ellie?" Casey asked snippin' away at the elderly woman's toenails. "Yer lookin' at it, Honey." The woman replied. "I sat right here and stared out this winda watchin' the world go by." Casey cut just a little bit off the middle toe. "Know what I did? I went and did just a little bit of exploring. I went out to that old school outside a town. Lawnwood School, ever heard of it?" Casey bit her lip and grabbed the file. "'Course I heard a it! My husband attended school out there. He was there the day it burned to the ground! That was quite the sumthin' ya know! 'Round here that sort a thing is big news. "Especially when somebody done gits killed." Casey stopped dead in her tracks and looked up at the old woman. "Somebody got killed out there?" Casey asked in wonder. "Oh yeah. 'Ole man Buell and that fancy Warner girl! Mr. Buell was a good man. He was our neighbor for a long while when we lived out on Robinson highway. I remember Daddy was so sad when he passed in that schoolhouse fire. We took a smoked ham to the widda. Don't poke me with that file now Honey, ya know I cain't feel nothin' in my feet!" She stopped and shook her head slowly from side to side. "Now that Warner girl was a looker and nice enough, put on airs though. You don't wanna see anyone die in a fire. Seems an awful way to go, don't it? They say ole' Eustice Buell's hands was burned clear to the bone when they found him. He was tossin' things around lookin' for that girl...never did find her body. " Casey reached for the lotion, squirting a hefty dollop in the palm of her hand. She sat quietly for a second as she rubbed lotion on Miss Ellie's dry feet and legs. "Yeah boy! I'd say it'd be an awful way."

"Ya know that woman that was the headmistress out there? That Miss Shay? She come into town and took over the job a City Manager after a piece. Strange woman...but she had some skills, I'd give her that. Honey can you rub some a that on my back? I'm feelin' a little scaly lately."

Chapter 8

The woodstove was poppin' and
snappin' a friendly tune as Casey and
Benj sat crosslegged on the sofa. It
was chilly outside but the old living
room was rich with the smell of good
seasoned wood and supper cookin'.
Around them were stacked piles and
piles of old newspapers. It had
become a ritual around this farm; on
Sunday evenings they would finish a
nice meal and trim the headlines off
Benj's unsold newspapers. They
worked quickly and mindlessly,
stacking the papers and rolling the
headlines in bundles of fifty. Benj
would return these bundles and get

reimbursed for them..so they ripped and rubber banded and talked peacefully. They were dressed in soft sweatpants and shirts, comfortable and happy. They laughed and talked about nothing like it was something and enjoyed each other as it should be.

"You've gotta tell those folks to quit sendin' you so many papers, Benj. Good God! It seems like more every week." Casey didn't mind helping Benj rip and sort. She actually kind of liked the quiet time together. "I do tell them! They don't listen. They just send what they want."

"Hey, did I tell you what Miss Ellie told me about the school?" said

Casey, deep in thought. "No, what?" replied Benj. "Somebody got killed in the fire out there." Casey rolled and banded another fifty headlines. "Hand me a few more a those rubber bands, will ya?" Benj tossed a box Casey's way. Her forehead crisscrossed and furrowed. "Why you lookin' so pensive?" Casey stopped dead and stared at her old friend. "I guess that makes sense." Benj said snappin' another bundle. "What makes sense?" Casey didn't move. "Well, since you see dead people and all." A slow smile crossed over Benj's face as she teased Casey. "I do not see dead people! I am not straight out of "The Sixth Sense"! Geez, Benj, don't

say that sorta crap! That upsets me."
Casey looked down at the mess of
papers in her lap. "I don't see dead
people, I don't." she muttered, mostly
to herself. "Okay, you don't out and
out see 'em but you have to admit
somethin' goes on, Case. Always has.
Why were you out there so long the
other day? Did you explore? Did you
poke through debris? You were really
clean when you came home." Benj
looked at Casey. "I'm not trying to
hurt your feelings Casey. But I know
this school thing is burrowing under
your skin and I want you to be
careful...that's all. What did you do
out there anyway?" Casey shuffled a
little, dropping a few papers on the

floor. "I sat on the step." Casey stalled "And I watched some kids raise the flag." She said quietly. "What? What kids? Casey there's no flag out there! That's nothing out there but an old dead hulk of a building...no kids, no flag. Damn it, Casey! Now I'm gonna have to go with you all the time."

"There is a flagpole, I found it. It's broken but it's there. Right there, where the kids were hoistin' it. Right where I saw it. I don't see dead people Benj. I'm never scared or upset or any of that. It's like a warm bath, with lavender...no, lilac." Benj sighed, "What difference does it make, lavender or lilac, I swear Casey, they're both purple flowers? Casey squinted. "I like lilac better. But it doesn't last." She glanced at Benj. "It's like a loop Benj. Like a recording stuck in a time warp. I don't know how it happens and I don't know why I can see it. It's like I fall out of time for a second. That's all it is..a slip, a little slip in time.

"Well, I'm sure it ain't sumthin' Jesus would want you up to!" said Benj in her very best Oklahoma accent. Casey gave her the fast stink eye and a big grin spread across her face. "Bless yer heart." Casey replied in her own perfect Okie accent.

Chapter 9

The elderly woman stared out the window of the nursing home. She was stuck in this place and resented every second. She rested her head against the back of her wheelchair and sighed heavily. She'd been feeling somewhat uneasy lately and had no idea why. She watched the cars and trucks zoom by on the highway just above the parking area. "How the hell did I end up here?" She murmured just loud enough to catch the attention of one of the staff.

"Can I help you, Miss Shay? Do you need anything? How 'bout I get you a juice box?" The young girl fawned.

Dorothea Shay waved her hand, dismissing the girl without a word. She sighed again watching the energetic girl scurry out of the day room. Miss Shay ran her dry, spotted hand over what was left of her hair. "Serves me right I suppose, endin' up in this place surrounded by everything I hate. Something is brewin' though...trouble comin'."

Chapter 10

"Honey put those books overn' that pile there by the door will ya? Thank ya, Baby." Benj loved volunteering at the library. She got a kick out of the librarian, Miss Constance, and the work was kinda fun. This woman had started the place back in the day and did everything herself. Lately, her biggest draw was the free video service; rarely did anyone actually take out a book anymore. But with her care the small town library kept plugging along under it's own steam. Miss Constance made sure of that.

The tiny woman was elderly and bent, but chugged with an energy most folk her age had tossed by the wayside years before. She had a smile for everyone and used it universally. She would set up demonstrations and shows for kids, cooking classes using healthy foods on a budget for Mamas, and still check out the occasional book. Benj looked at Miss Constance as a powerhouse of the community and loved spending time with her.

That day as lunchtime rolled around Benj was starting to feel the workout her elderly friend was putting her through. She was cleaning shelves and hefting books and trying hard to clean up some of the mess the old library held. Benj had gotten the idea to volunteer her services when she came in to have something notarized and had almost tripped across the floor on a pile of something.

Benj loved the old dusty feel of the place and the slight musty smell of the books. These days most folks rarely made it past the front where Miss Constance had the movies neatly displayed. But to Benj the mystery was in the dark shelves of old books no one touched anymore. She had found some amazing things tucked away in those long forgotten nooks and crannies.

It was like a time capsule to Benj and even though she wasn't as apt to admit it as Casey , she was still drawn into the forgotten past.

Whenever she had a second or two to rub together Benj would find herself pokin' around the old sections of the building. She would walk, lightly touching the leather bound books, reading their names like taking a stroll through a cemetery. Some of the books she found would call out and touch her heart. Some were just fun and silly, grossly outdated and amusing. Books on etiquette and long ago dismissed ideas of health and well being. Benj would find an old tome and plop

herself down in the dust and
dishevelment to pore over the
wisdom long gone. She would slowly
munch her sandwich and chuckle or
wonder over her findings.

Benj slid down to the dusty floor
and opened her lunch. She loved a
good ham sandwich and she was
ready for this one. Her first bite just
melted away in her mouth as she
closed her eyes and savored the
smoky flavor. A short sip of water and
she was ready. She reached out and
touched the shelf in front of her. Oh,
how she loved the feel of leather
bound books. Years ago she had
watched a ninety year old woman
hand bind a book in soft, beautiful

leather and Benj's thoughts on bookbinding were forever changed. She let her knuckles scuff lightly over the spines in front of her. Her dirty face was a perpetual grin as she chose a book of the day. As she pulled her chosen book from the shelf, a faded paper came along with it. This happened all the time. People sticking papers and notes in the books and leaving them behind to be found years later. Benj always wondered about the writer of them, usually school kids. The paper was pink, faded. It was folded in half and almost hidden. She smiled as she opened it. It was an old flyer. "Chili Dinner And Pie Sale" it proclaimed.

"Come One, Come All!" "Pies will be auctioned by our own bank Manager Willard Stout. All proceeds will go directly to the Athletic Department Of Lawnwood School for the purchase of new uniforms for the Basketball Team!"

Benj dropped the paper. She couldn't believe her eyes. What were the chances of finding this paper now? When Casey was fallin' into some sort of fit over that old carcass of a school! Benj heard the front door open and Miss Constance call out for her. "Damn!" She muttered. She didn't even get to finish her sandwich. Benj worked her way to her feet and hurried down the stairs to meet the smilin' face of her friend.

"Lordy Honey you look like you seen a ghost up there in those stacks! What's the matter with ya?" Miss Constance looked concerned as Benj handed her the pink paper. "You know anything about this old school, Ma'am?" Miss Constance pulled her desk chair over and sat down hard. "O' course I do Honey. I was there the day it burned."

Chapter 11

Benj coughed and almost choked so she swilled from the bottle of water she was holding. "You were there?" she almost screamed. "Well, yes Honey. My Daddy worked for Philpro Oil, so me and my two brothers attended Lawnwood School just like everyone else out there." Benj plopped herself in the nearest chair and asked. "Can you tell me anything about it?" Benj was as wide eyed as a child and Miss Constance was a bit amused by the whole thing. "It was a lovely school, Honey. All stone and clean. We were all so proud of it. We all did our part to make it as good as it could be. Like that pie auction in the flyer there. We had goings on like that all the time. We had a regular little community out there. It was a nice place to grow up. Terrible when the school burned though." Miss Constance put her head down and fiddled with a frayed ribbon on her desk blotter. "I lost my best friend that day in that fire Honey...Becky Warner and I was thick as thieves back then." She took another tug at the ribbon. "I guess no matter how old a body gets you jus don't lose track a somethin' like that do ya? Lord, I remember that day like I was there right now. I could tell ya every word we said, every thing we saw. It was an awful day, Honey. You best just stay away from that place. I believe God himself has stepped away from there. Benj rested her chin in the palm of her hand and watched the old woman. "Casey and I have been doin' some research on that old hulk out there. Well , Casey mostly. Would you be willing to have a talk with her?" Benj asked hopefully.

"Why sure I'll talk to Casey! I like that girl and I like how she cares for Mrs. Ebert out on Old 75. She thinks the world a that girl I'll tell you what!" Benj could barely contain her excitement. "Oh Man! She is gonna be so excited to hear all this! She's taken some sort of jones about that place and well, she loves a good story in the first place!" Benj raised her hands and said "When?" The elderly woman beamed "Oh Honey, anytime. I love to talk about the old days. That school may not be the best memory this ole' head is stuck with but it is history, ain't it. Ya know...I've got some boxes with most the stuff they salvaged from the fire packed away somewhere in this ole' library. They had it all in the old Police Department but when they tore that down no one knew what to do with the stuff. I hope I didn't throw it away. I don't want to be lyin' to ya now." Benj sat with her mouth hangin' open. The taste for her

ham sandwich completely gone.
"We've gotta find it." She said.

Chapter 12

"Do you believe all that Case?" Benj had almost jumped down Casey's throat as she walked in the door that evening. She had much to tell Casey and excitement bubbled from her like a fountain.

Casey looked slightly pensive as she flopped herself on the sofa. "Well, it pretty much makes sense that a lot of folks would be out there at the time of the fire I guess." Casey scratched her head and sighed. She glanced around the cozy room and picked up a cat to snuggle. "It was a public school and that old oil plant was a boomin' business at the time. I guess we shouldn't be surprised that folks are gonna be aware, even though they are all pretty old." Casey sat the cat on the coffee table and stretched out on the sofa, kicking her shoes across the room.

"Why you getting so comfortable?" Benj asked, watching Casey relax. "What about supper? I didn't even get to eat my sandwich today I was in such a tizzy over this school thing! I'm about starved to death!" Benj pleaded. Casey smiled and dropped her arm over her eyes. "Wanna run into town for some gas station food tonight?" Casey asked without moving.

Suddenly Casey dropped her arm and half sat up. "You know, finding any info on the internet about that school or the fire is near impossible. I've Googled! There's nothin'! It's like one of those things that happen in town and just stays here." Casey cocked her head and looked at Benj. "Sometimes I just don't understand this small town living thing. Everybody knows everything about everyone but it's all hush, hush and under the table outside of town limits! Really weird. Don't worry Benj..." Casey yawned and sat up. "Supper's on the way. Why don't you get the dogs fed and I'll make some biscuits. You feel like some tuna melts tonite?" Benj shuffled toward the back door. "Kinda have a taste for some fried okra. Can we have some a that along with the tuna melts?" Casey smiled just a little. She loved that Benj enjoyed her cooking but man, tonight she was tired. Okra only came once a year though and it wouldn't be long before this seasonal delight would turn woody on the vine. Casey washed her hands in the chipped old sink and started slicing the plump little pods.

Stanley Dover pruned his roses in the ever increasing shadows the setting sun cast. He carefully snipped and talked softly to his tender shoots. For as long as he could remember he had been a teacher at the public school here in town. He had a little house right across the street from the red brick schoolhouse. It seemed fitting he should live the end of his life here in the shadow of this institution. He had spent almost sixty years walking those varnished halls. He would sit on the porch on warm days and let the sun sink into his old bones. He would smile and wave to the children as they passed. He could almost remember the faces, almost remember the reason why he was here. It didn't matter much anyhow. There was a woman that showed up every day and left him tasty food to eat and made sure he was clean and his house tidy. She would remind him what day they were on and maybe what year. Stanley had a hard time remembering these things on his own. But he still loved to watch the children. So he waved and smiled his toothless smile in the kindly way old men did. The kids would giggle and wave back knowing full well that was Mr. Dover...the Social Studies Teacher. He had taught their parents and their grandparents alike. He was famous around here. The kids would laugh and snicker "crazy ole' man" behind his back but he never knew that, for Stanley Dover was a happy man; he had everything he needed...

as the memories of his life slowly slipped from his grasp.

Chapter 13

Casey pulled her truck up along side Benj's little silver car. "Hey!" She yelled rolling down her window. "Need a ride little girl?" Casey waggled her eyebrows up and down in the most perverted way she could think of. Benj sat next to a big oak tree looking dejected and unsmiling. She slowly got to her feet and dusted herself off. "Did you bring the gas can?" she snapped at Casey. "Of course I did! That's what you told me to do." Casey smiled and tried to lighten Benj's cloudy mood, it wasn't working. Benj grabbed the half filled plastic container from the back of the truck and started dumping it in her bone dry gas tank. "Look at this car, Casey!" Benj yelled. "It's missing two hubcaps, the brakes are shot, it's filthy and it was a brand new vehicle when I got out here! I just can't maintain it! I can't maintain anything out here...there's just not enough money." Benj laid her forehead on the roof of the little car, "I feel bad about that, Case." she said softly. "I'm behind in my bills. The little car I've been so proud of is shot to shit and I just don't know what to do." Benj swiped her hand over her eyes. "I love it out here. This is my dream life." She turned her head toward Casey. "I don't know man, I just don't know. Something has to give...it just has to."

Casey stared at her, fingers wrapped around the steering wheel. She knew in her heart if something major went wrong with her truck it would be a horrible disaster. There just wasn't any money. She glanced at Benj and her heart broke. She wanted for all the world for her friend to be happy. She deserved to be happy! And when the garden grew and there were buckets of fresh tomatoes and cucumbers she saw a happiness on Benj she had never seen before. When the lambs were born and they canned jams and jellies together she knew Benj was the only one that understood this life. This strange and wonderful and sometimes awful life.

Choppin' wood and cold water showers. Bad storms and faulty septic. It was all a part of living on the edge of nowhere. She watched with a tear in her eye as Benj emptied the gas can and tossed it back in the truck. She thought of Christmas, making ornaments out of pine cones and cutting down a cedar to decorate. It was a good life. And it was all just a little more fun with Benj by her side.

Benj ducked her head in Casey's window. "Stop with the tears! Why do you have to be so sensitive!" Benj touched Casey's shoulder. "We'll be okay. I'm just pissed right now,

Case...by the time I drive into town and home it'll all be over." Benj cracked a little smile. "There better be a good supper on that table though!" She slapped Casey's truck and sprinted over to her car. Casey watched in the rear view mirror as Benj cranked the engine and gave her the thumbs up. "I hope it's okay Benj, I really do." Casey muttered to herself.

Chapter 14

"Yoohoo! Miss Casey! Miss Casey!"
Casey squinted into the rising sun
trying hard to figure out who was
yoohooing her so early on a Monday
morning. "Oh my lands, Miss Casey! I
been tryin' to git in touch with you or
my little Benj for the last month or
so! Library's been closed so I haven't
seen Benj! You know that ole' sewer
line that the CCC laid way back in the
1930's, well, I don't know how the
uppity ups in this town thought that
was gonna last forever! I swan Honey,
the stink in that library was somethin'
that could choke a mule for awhile
there! They done tore up the whole

crawlspace and north wall! It's fixed now, thank Jesus! I've had people out the door tryin' to git movies to watch day after day. You know there ain't a lick a entertainment in this town proper!" Miss Constance finally took breath. Casey blinked.

"So, the library is fixed now? Benj can come back to help you again?" Casey asked, trying not to open another floodgate of conversation. "Why yes! I'd love to have Benj back agin! She is such a pleasure and what a help! I don't know what I did before she came around! But the big thing I wanted to tell y'all is when we was tearin' things up I found those boxes a stuff from the fire! You know...the

Lawnwood School fire! Thought they was lost forever but there they were, big as life! Now, you tell Benj to come on over and we can have a sit down will ya now? She was very interested in all that mess." Casey blinked again. Miss Constance could run her ragged but the mention of the treasures left her stunned. "'Course I will Miss Constance...'course I will."

That afternoon just before the sun gave up the day Casey pulled her truck in the long forgotten driveway of Lawnwood School. The shadows cast by the masonry were long and more than a little chilling. It hadn't been a cold winter but Casey had been concerned that the old schoolhouse had tumbled to rubble over the past months. As she stared up at the vacant windows and elegant archways she was thrilled to see nothing was a minute worse for wear.

Casey strolled down the sidewalk that ran the front of the building. She kicked away a small portion of dead weeds that had almost hidden the old pathway. Under the overgrowth she saw signs of the children that were once there. Old and worn and barely readable were initials carved over a half century before. Pocket knives and fountain pens had made their marks in the sidewalks there. Names and letters carved by students long dead, declaring their love, or friendship, or just simply who they were. She made her way to the wide steps and gazed into the front door. Somewhere in the back of her mind she heard a bell toll. She was gonna be late! The bell pounded in the back of her skull. Class was gonna start...oh my, she was gonna catch hell if she was late again! Ole' Miss Shay would ship her home and Daddy would tan her hide for sure! Casey rushed into the building. She felt the crush of kids making their way to class around her. They all smiled and said "Howdy!" to one another. They clapped each other on the backs and laughed at secret jokes among them. The wide wood plank floors creaked under the feet of a hundred bustling kids. She looked down at her bobby socks and black Mary Janes. Babbling away right by her side were her best friends. "We best move it 'fore Miss Shay chews our butts...again!" Connie rolled her eyes and grabbed her hand. They swung around the corner and into the classroom just as the bell stopped its discord. The black clad woman at the front of the room turned and placed her hands on her hips. Her lip curled slightly as she looked the girls up and down. "Well, good of you to join us today, Miss Warner. And almost on time..."

Casey shook her head and took her hand from the warm stone wall. Her breath was comin' hard, like she was runnin' for a train. Her hand shook as she ran it nervously through her hair. Casey made her way out of the building. "Wow, that's further in than I've ever made it. Progress maybe." She suddenly felt weak as a kitten and sat down hard on the front steps. "Maybe not." She sighed. Casey sat and wondered at the beauty of this place. The ruins overlooked a pond surrounded by cattle munching on newly grown grass. She picked and poked at the cement, running her fingers over the pale writings there.

Before long she'd found a little verse scratched into the old masonry...

C.B.

E.B.

B.W.

Friends until the Canadian River has to wear diapers to keep it's bottom dry!

Chapter 15

Spring was a fleeting thing out on the grasslands and summer with its oppressive heat and humidity made it's way through the plains far too soon. Casey pushed her damp, sweaty hair back from her face. Her old Toyota truck didn't feature any sort of air conditioning so every degree was felt and noticed.

"Okay that's it, I've had it!" Casey swung the little truck into the local beauty shop and bounded up the stairs. "Hey Miss Cheryl! You got any time to snip this mess off a me today?" Casey asked the little town's one and only beautician/barber. Miss Cheryl lowered her glasses and gave Casey the once over. "Sweet Jesus on a raft Honey, it's a wonder you ain't expired with that head a hair on you in this balmy weather. Sit yerself down and I'll get to you directly. Casey plopped herself in one of the chairs topped with a honeycomb dryer. "Can I sit here Miss Cheryl?" Cheryl waved her hand never missin' a snip.

Y'all heard ole' Stanley Dover was walkin' around in the school in his pajamas agin din't ya?" shouted Mrs. Talula Fry over the sounds of the dryers. "I did hear that...bless his heart...poor man ain't got a brain cell left to get lonely does he? I have to wonder why no one's put him up in a nursin' home yet?" replied Miss Cheryl.

"Well, the school board gave him that little house over there back a the playin' field. He was a teacher for so long they figured he earned it." Mrs. Fry announced. "Yeah, I know all that, but the man just ain't right anymore, poor soul." Both ladies shook their heads and muttered "bless him" under their breaths. "He ain't got kin, poor feller. He's there on his own." Miss Cheryl said, carefully trimming Mrs. Fry's bangs.

Casey listened with interest as her overheated body started to return to a semi-normal temperature. "Hey Miss Cheryl, can I get a water while I'm waitin'? I'll pay you back in a bit." Casey asked. "Oh Honey, that's what it's there for! Help yer self!" Miss Cheryl shouted without raising her eyes. "Hey y'all, is that Stanley Dover you're talkin' about the same guy used to teach out at the Lawnwood School?" Casey asked, snappin' the seal and takin' a long drink.

"I don't know." both women chimed up. "Sure could be, he's been around these parts forever and a day! Knock on Viola's dryer there...she'd prolly know." Casey tapped lightly on the roaring dryer covering the head of one of her favorite elderly women.

"Oh hey, Baby!" Miss Viola grinned from ear to ear as she started awake from her dryer-induced sleep. "Hey Miss Viola! It's so good to see you again!" Casey smiled and took the lady's hand. "Oh Baby, I sure enough didn't see you come in here...you was quiet!" Casey once again tapped the dryer and shouted..."No Miss Viola, you was loud!" "I was snoozin' is what I was doin'! Gittin' my hair fixed always has put me right into a stupor!" Casey grinned. She loved this woman to the ends of time. She had experienced a terrible farm accident several years earlier and Casey had been her caretaker. They had developed a strong bond between them. "Miss Viola did you go to school out at Lawnwood?" shouted Cheryl. "Well no...I went out to Long Creek. Why you askin'?" Miss Viola settled in her chair. "Casey was wonderin' if Stanley Dover used to teach out there 'fore he came to town, that's why!" said Cheryl, expertly twisting a curling iron. "Oh yeah, if I recall correctly, he did teach out there. Came to town after the fire a course. He was a popular teacher out there just like he was here."

Cheryl stuck a comb in her mouth and motioned Miss Viola to get back under the dryer. "She ain't never gonna git dry she don't stay under there! She likes all them tight curls...hard to set."

"Mrs. Fry?" Casey asked. "Were you out there when the schoolhouse burned?" The old woman closed her eyes and let her chin drop just a little. "No Casey I wasn't out there but I sure remember the ruckus it all caused. I remember Daddy comin' home that evenin' covered in soot and smellin' awful. My Daddy was a volunteer fireman back then and well, everyone in the county showed up to help that afternoon. Viola's daddy was out there as well. It was such a cold and snowy afternoon. It all seems like a dream now, don't it, Viola?" They all glanced at the woman under the dryer. She was softly snoozin' again, holding Casey's hand.

"Viola! Viola! Wake up! We're havin' a conversation here and you need to participate! Viola!" Cheryl stomped her foot and Miss Viola started awake. "What!" She mumbled liftin' the dryer from her damp head. "Were you out at the Lawnwood fire? I swear to heaven sometimes havin' a simple conversation 'round here is like pullin' teeth from somebody's head!" Casey stifled a chuckle and turned to Miss Viola.

"Daddy packed us all up in the Chevy and drove us out to see if we could be any help I guess. Sometimes I think all this "help" people are offerin' is just birth to a bunch a looky-lous. But yeah, we went out. Mama packed us in with a pile a those ole' rubber hot water bottles and off we went. We found Jeffy Pile wanderin' down the road, so we put him in the car and got him warm. Later we drove him home to his family; they was grateful. I remember the roof was caved by the time we got there so I guess Mr. Buell had already met his maker. It was a sad day all around. I had a little crush on Jeffy Pile though so I was glad to be helpin' him and his people. I remember that strange Shay woman glidin' all over the place though. I was a kid and I sure didn't wanna come up aginst her,

I'll tell ya." Miss Viola sat back again. "She still alive?" asked Cheryl. "Ain't heard she's dead." Said Mrs. Fry "She's still alive!" proclaimed Casey. "Good Lord, how old is she now?"

"Well Honey she wasn't that much older'n those teen girls back then. She looked older cause she dressed like a nun or an Amish...weird woman...she always scared me!" You git back under that dryer Viola, I'd like to go home sometime tonite!" Cheryl scolded. "Yeah, I think she's still holed up in that nursing home out on the highway ain't she?" Piped in Mrs. Fry. "I believe so now that you mention it. I never liked when she was Town Commissioner; always had the fake smile. Casey git up here! Takes me an hour to cut that head a hair a yourn, I best git to it!" Casey jumped up on demand and settled in the well versed hands of Miss Cheryl.

Chapter 16

"Ya went and saw Miss Cheryl I see!" Exclaimed Benj as she shuffled into the kitchen sniffin' the air with every breath. She made her way to the stove and started liftin' lids to see what was for supper. "You lift that lid on the rice and I'll shoot you." Casey said carelessly, not even turning to look. "God woman! You got eyes everywhere!" Benj reached out and touched Casey's shorn 'do. "I like it! It was getting a little shaggy you know." Casey shook her head. "I do know...that's why I got it cut." Casey turned from the sink and smiled at Benj. "You could stand an hour or two with Miss Cheryl yourself sometime soon. How was your day?" "It was good. I cut and stacked that wood we got up on Gopher Ridge last Sunday. Got about half a rick, nice wood too. Good, solid oak. What's for supper?" Casey pulled up a cucumber she was washing and waved it at Benj. "Mr. Dunbar's brother-in-law came into town with a pile of garden goods today and he gave me some. So...you get that cucumber salad you love so much. Get your dirty hands off my fresh biscuits! Go wash...supper's almost on the table."

After their bellies were full of fresh garden greens, Casey and Benj settled in for the evening. "Wanna go out on the porch and watch the sunset?" Benj asked Casey, sighing happily and pattin' her belly. "Sure I do! Do you think that raccoon's been back eatin' the cat food again?" asked Casey as she rolled off the sofa and picked up her homemade house slippers. "Maybe so. Maybe if we sit in the dark it'll come on up. Benj grinned. "Yeah, then what do we do smartypants? said Casey, swatting at Benj with a slipper. "Sit quietly." answered Benj.

It was a soft, velvety night on the Oklahoma prairie as the two women sat staring off into the brilliant party the sun was throwing as it made its escape for yet another day.

"If you sit real still just like this you can almost slip in and out of any time you want to can't you?" Casey mused. "Well, you can." whispered Benj. "I'm afraid I don't have those particular abilities, Casey."

"No, I mean just look around. There's not a thing in this soft night that has changed so much since say, oh, the turn of the century." Casey rocked back in her chair, "See, look across the pasture there. Think about the family that first came here and first cleared and turned that land. Man, what a job that had to have been!" Casey sipped her sweet tea and swatted a bug away from her face. "I'll bet it smelled different though. No cars or trucks or oil wells stinkin' up the place." Benj glanced over at Casey's dreamy face. "Well, I'll bet the people smelled different, that's pretty much for certain. No hot, runnin' water, no deodorant...no Coast soap." Benj teased. "Yeah, you're probably right. Hey, did Miss Constance ever find that box of stuff from the school?" Casey turned her head and could just make out the outline of her friend's face. "Oh shit! I forgot to tell you! Yeah, she found it when they tore up the sewer line. Geez, Case, I'm sorry! I should have told you. She said we can come in anytime to poke through that stuff." Casey shivered in spite of the warm summer night. "Cool! When?" She asked.

Chapter 17

It was a white hot day on this particular Saturday morning. The kind of day that singed the hairs in your nostrils breathin' in. Main Street looked like a bomb threat had been announced and no one told Casey or Benj as they strolled toward the library. Not a heartbeat was to be found, human or otherwise. "Man it's hot! I wonder where the rest a the town got off to on this sultry morning?" asked Benj. Casey shook her head and cupped her hand over her eyes. "It's freaky hot out here! Everything looks so sharp and breakable." Benj glanced at her friend. "Yeah, kinda does...I guess that's a pretty good way to describe it." Suddenly the silence was broken by the slam of a door and a shout. "Miss Casey! Miss Casey!" Casey spun around to face the granddaughter of one of her clients. "Hi Shelly Ann, what's up?" she asked. "Y'all goin' overt' the pancake breakfast at the High School this mornin'?" The woman asked hopefully. "Oh geez!" exclaimed Casey. "I forgot all about that pancake breakfast! No, we're goin' over to meet Miss Constance at the library. Why do you ask?" "Oh, I was hopin' to hitch a ride with ya's all. Guess I'm gonna have to jist wait on Howard then. Have a good time at the library...tell Miss Constance 'Hey' for me now. You know she goes to the Pancake Breakfast but she gets there at the crack a dawn, poor soul. Y'all take care now!" Casey and Benj watched as Shelly Ann scurried back down the street.

"Why is Miss Constance a poor soul?" mused Benj. "No tellin'. I think she's pretty happy if you ask me." Casey kicked a stray rock down the deserted street. "Me too." said Benj.

The heavy brass door of the library opened with a swish and a flood of cold, crisp air bathed the girls. Both sighed a heavy sigh of relief as they entered the cool, dark foyer. "Hey girls, throw the bolt on that door will ya? I don't want anybody wanderin' in. The library's closed and I don't want anybody gittin' surly 'cause they cain't check out a movie to watch!" Benj did what she was told and the women wandered in to the familiar room. They were wrapped in the wonderful smell of old leather bindings and paper and freon. Miss Constance had the air cranked and the dimly lit room felt invitingly cool. Suddenly from out of nowhere Miss Constance appeared. "Damn, Miss Constance I can't see a thing in here comin' from the outside! Sure feels good though." said Benj. "Oh, give it jist a second and you'll be fine,

Honey. Got it kinda chilled in here, don't I? I like it though. I cain't take the heat anymore. You should feel it at my house, I swear you could hang meat in my livin' room! I jist came from the Pancake Breakfast. Those boys know how to turn a sausage! I go every year....look forward to it. Did you make it over there?" "No, Miss Heavner called and said she had extra tickets but we had to drop the truck off over't LeRoy's so we walked on from there." explained Casey. "Oh Honey, you need to go one year! It's a good plate a food, that's for certain. Well, come on girls let's git to those boxes! It's such a mess back here! Those fellas done tore up this whole back wall lookin' for that leak! I'm hopin' I can persuade Miss Benj here to come by next week and give me a hand cleanin' some of this up!" Miss Constance nodded Benj's way with a little grin. "Well, twist my arm, Ma'am! You know I'd be happy to do that!" Benj replied. "I know Honey, I can always count on you."

As they ventured further back in the building, the smell of sewer became more and more noticeable. The women pushed past a mountain of stray books and papers and got the first glimpse of the damage the leak had caused. The back wall was patched with new concrete and the floor was uneven and bowed. "Them boys caused more damage than the leak, I swan!" said Miss Constance shaking her head. "This town and its water problems. You know what the problem is, don'cha? They built the whole system back just after the Land Run! Nothin' lasts forever! They got a good long ride outta this ole' clay pipe system but it's just shot. No one up ta City Hall gonna agree with that though...just keep patchin'. That should be their motto. They should write that on those fancy new cruisers they're sportin' around town. Just Keep Patchin'" The old woman shook her head in disgust. "Anyhoo! Ain't mine to say. Here's those boxes right here girls!" She pointed at the two medium-sized boxes sittin' at her feet. "They ain't heavy. Both a you two grab one and we can take em' up front where the stink ain't so cloyin'.

Chapter 18

Benj reached down and hefted one of the boxes. Noddin' her head at Casey. "Grab that one, girlfriend, we can look through them up in the front." Casey grabbed the remaining box and the little party started for the better lit section of the library. "Boy, if this is all that was left after the fire it sure didn't leave much did it?" Benj scooted her box on to one of the long wooden tables with the old fashioned green shaded lamps mounted to the sides. "No Honey, once the roof give in there wasn't much left to say I'm afraid. Miss Casey put that right there ta the side." They all stared at the old cardboard crates. Across the top was written "Lawnwood School", the boxes were the file sort with lids and handles and thankfully they were treated with some sort of wax coating so the recent water damage didn't touch them.

"Well alrighty then!" said Benj as she popped the top from the first box. Inside carefully wrapped in crumbling newspapers were trophies. The air wafting from them smelled of smoke and disaster. The trophies were charred and some had cracks from the heat on that fateful day so long ago. Under the tarnished Loving Cups and brass plaques lay a banner made of felt and satin. It was a faded dark red and gold. "Those were the school colors back then." Miss Constance muttered. Casey reached out her hand and softly touched the edge of crumbled material. "Oh, I remember the basketball games...." Casey's fingertips closed around the old banner.

The boy sat quietly on the side of the roadway. It was hot and still for this time of the year. Normally in November the trees were already turnin' and you could feel a breath of fall in the air. But this year had been unseasonably warm and that Oklahoma heat just wasn't ready to give up on itself quite yet. The boy had been walkin' these back roads for awhile and he was feelin' steamy and tired. From this cozy rock a his he could make out a crystal clear little pond through the timbers. He was so tempted to take a stroll on down there and take a dip...but he had to be back on base in three days and Lawton seemed a long way down the road. Finally he stood up, stretched his long legs and ran his fingers over the buzz cut the Army had so thoughtfully bestowed upon him. Before long he stripped off his khaki shirt and tied the sleeves around his skinny waist. Once again he started his walk down the roadway. He knew his schedule was tight but he'd spent his bus fare on some pretty little girl during his home visit and now he had to hoof it back to base. It had been worth it though. They had danced the night away and before the sun rose he'd gotten a kiss or two, so he was a happy boy that warm November day. Before he knew it his luck held steady and a car came putterin' around the bend. The car was a convertible, dark blue with wide white walls; every boy's dream car. The kid stuck out a thumb and sure enough if that car didn't pull right over! The lanky boy ran to open the door and was greeted by a young guy much like himself. Skinny with dark hair and an easy smile. "Where you headin', Soldier?"

the guy asked. "Tryin' hard to git back to Fort Sill 'fore Friday." the boy stated, tryin' hard to get his shirt back on and his pack in the car all at the same time. "You don't need to bother with that shirt kid...I got cloth seats"....

"Casey! Casey!" Casey opened her eyes to Benj's worried face just inches from hers. "Casey! Damn it! You with us?" Casey tried to push herself up. "Yeah, get off me, Benj! Geez!" "I'm callin' 911! Don't know what good it'd do, those boys are all at the Pancake Breakfast stuffin' their faces." Casey heard in the background somewhere. "I'm fine! Don't y'all dare call 911 and ruin those folks' day! Let me up...I'm okay!" Casey sputtered. "I'll bet it's her blood sugar. Honey, you been tested for the sugar diabetes? So many people come down with the sugar diabetes around here." Miss Constance shoved her face close to Casey's. "No Miss Constance, I don't have diabetes! I think it was the walk in the sun and the sewer smell. Lord, let me up Benj!" Benj stood worriedly staring at her friend. "You never passed out before Casey." Benj said softly. "I never walked around in 100 degree heat then stuck my nose in sewer gas before either! God!! I'm fine." Casey crawled to her feet and dusted herself off. "What'd I just drop over? She asked. "Yes!" Both women exclaimed in unison. "Benj, I think I best go home now. Miss Constance I still wanna see those boxes. Can we make it another time? Casey pleaded. "They ain't goin' nowhere girl. I cain't open the library till the stink wears down so I ain't gonna touch em'. They gonna sit right there where we're leavin' em'. Come on now...git her home Benj!" Benj nodded, still lookin' panicked. "Go get the truck from LeRoy and meet me out front, will ya?" Benj nodded. "Oh Benj, I'm fine. Get that look off your puss and go get the truck." In a matter of minutes Benj got Casey settled in the front seat of the truck. Benj turned to her friend. "Okay, what did you see?"

Chapter 19

"It didn't have anything to do with the school!" Casey sighed as she flopped back in bed. Benj had insisted she 'go to bed' the second they rolled the truck into the lane. Casey had to admit she was beat and baffled as she slid between her fresh clean sheets. "Oh Jesus, Case, you know it had something to do with it. You just don't know what yet. I have to tell you I'm getting' just a little tired of the whole thing. I mean I'm intrigued that's true, but if it's gonna mean you're droppin' over all over the place, I can't say I'm for all that. "I didn't 'drop over all over the place" pouted Casey. "Yeah, ya did! You didn't see it! It was freaky as hell! Your eyes rolled back in your head! I know that sounds like an old cliché but it happened Casey! I almost puked! I thought you were havin' a seizure! Geez God! Don't ever do that shit again!" Benj threw her hands over her head and tried hard to keep from crying. "I can't take it! You are over your head in this thing and it has to stop!" Benj looked pleadingly at her pale friend.

"I'm just not sure it can stop...that's the problem here, Benj.' Casey said softly laying her hand over her friend's. "I agree I might be over my head but there's someone or something that seems to think I can handle all this...that we can handle all this, Benj. Not sure we can stop that." Casey tried to explain to Benj exactly what she had experienced. "Is it like a movie? Like you're watchin' on a screen?" asked Benj, concern seeping through her voice. "Sorta, only much more real....like you're actually there. I mean, there's no difference between that and real life. It's just like real life Benj. You can feel the breeze and smell the summer around you." Casey explained. "The thing is I've never had it happen so vividly before! I mean...well, you know. I "feel" things...but this is very different. And I hope it stops." Casey hung her head and a tear trickled onto the front of her t-shirt. "It's very uncomfortable Benj, but I know someone had to have left a lot of energy hangin' around for me to have this sort of reaction."

Casey wanted to talk but her eyes were heavy. "Sleep now." muttered Benj. "Hey, you want me to cook supper tonight?" One of Casey's eyes popped open in shock. "Yeah...how 'bout some of that baked spaghetti you make so well." Casey smiled as the door closed. "Okay". Benj whispered.

When Casey woke the room was dark. If she didn't hear the TV going in the living room she would have sworn she slept the entire night. She laid quietly, snugglin' deeply under the old quilt. Her kitty Ruby, swatted her for moving. She could hear Benj rattlin' pots and pans in the kitchen and knew there would be a mess to clean up. Benj didn't cook much but her baked pasta was comforting and very good.

Casey knew Benj was worried and Lord knows she had enough on her mind without Casey tumblin' over at random. Casey thought about what she'd seen when she'd passed out. It was all clear as glass in her mind. Not one bit like a dream. She could feel the soft warm breeze and smell the car exhaust. It was like she was there...right there. Casey ran her hand over her face and moved Ruby from her perch. She flipped on the bed light and pulled those homemade slippers over her feet. "Benj!" She shouted. "You better not be makin' a mess out there! Smells good though! Supper ready?"

Chapter 20

Casey steadied the old gentleman as he walked from the bedroom. She gently sat him in his chair and laid a towel over the blue velveteen arm of the well worn recliner. She draped another towel around his neck and pulled a kitchen chair close. She squeezed out a wash rag in a bowl of warm water perched on the chair and placed it carefully over his face.

Mr. Dunbar enjoyed it when Casey shaved him. She was careful and did a fine job. He was always particular about his looks and kept himself sparklin' clean. As he'd gotten older it became harder and harder to maintain his perfect hygiene on his own and Casey had handled things discreetly and with confidence. "Did you get any more information on that ole' schoolhouse out there past Greasy Creek? He muttered between strokes of the razor. "Oh my goodness, I've found out all sorts a things. I had no idea so many people around here attended school there!" said Casey, wiping a bit of foam off his nose. "My, my yes! This town used to be boomin' back during the oil rush. Ya know we had a big prisoner a war camp out Lake Road, din't ya?" He asked tippin' his head. Casey nodded. "Oh yes this place was somethin' back then! Me and Cora used to drive the car up to Main Street on Saturday afternoons, then walk on home just so we would have good parkin' for later! It was a lovely place.

Folks would put on a coat and tie to come to town on Saturday nights...." a misty look crossed his face. "I can just see my Cora decked out in a pretty dress and a hat all excited to see this picture show or the next. Then we'd pile up in the car and drive on out to the lake to steal a kiss or two." The old man shook his head.

"They was good times Casey. I came back from the War and we married right away. Lived in this town our whole lives. Never thought I'd lose her before me." He dropped his head and discreetly wiped at his eye. "We was a pretty good match, Cora and me...yeah, a pretty good match."

Casey gently wiped his face and put the shaving things aside. "Was she from here as well? she asked. "Oh yes, born and raised." A tiny smile crossed his face "I was an 'older man' ya know." He looked at Casey with a mischievous wink. " I was twenty five, she was only nineteen. Oh, her parents studied on that some, I'll tell you. But they ended up warmin' up to me after all." Casey smiled and patted his hand. "You dog, you!" He laughed. "Ya know what the worse thing for me was?" Mr. Dunbar hung his head and and kicked his foot out at his recliner. "It was havin' to put Mama in that nursin' home out there by the highway. Came the time I just couldn't look after her when the cancer took her so deep. Oh, I was out there ever day and even stayed some nights but it ain't the same as dyin' in yer own bed, now is it?

That's what I'm plannin' on doin' ya know?" He looked up and smiled a beautiful smile at Casey. "I'm awful glad I got you, Miss Casey. Reckon I'll have you 'til the end now won't I?" Casey patted his hand again. "I hope so, Sir. I really hope so."

Mr. Dunbar lowered his head and closed his eyes. Casey knew he'd be sound asleep in a matter of seconds. She softly pulled her hand out from his and patted him softly. She took the dirty shaving water and dumped it down the sink. This was the second time someone had mentioned that nursing home out by the highway.... Maybe she ought take a drive out there one day soon, just to take a look.

Chapter 21

Casey loved her little Toyota truck. It was messy and filled with her paperwork. She always called it her "mobile office." But time and again it refused to fail her. She was skirtin' 300,000 miles now and still the little white truck kept putterin' along.

Casey had bought a can of tractor paint several years earlier and given the little truck a makeover...with a paintbrush, but none were the wiser. The heater worked in winter and it rolled down the road; that was all that mattered.

Casey was flyin' down highway 27 with the windows open and the whole world had a happy slant. This road was one she loved to travel. Comin' off the ridge was one of the prettiest views you could imagine. The only thing that reminded you what century you were travelin' in was the odd appearance of the Vo-Tech dropped at the bottom of the draw.

It was a tidy little campus that taught kids and adults how to weld and plumb and fix a car. How to be nurses and care for folks in the last days of their lives. The Vo-Tech was a boon to this area and folks rarely studied elsewhere.

On either side of this little two lane highway were long abandoned peanut fields. The old peanut equipment sat rusting and silent like sentinels to a more prosperous day. Casey never really knew why peanuts went bust here. This was once the biggest peanut producer in America, then it was gone. But, here sat the fields, green and lush. Waiting for those noisy machines and the families that ran them. Waiting 'til the fields themselves reclaimed the steel and rubber.

Casey drove happily along watchin' the cattle and enjoying the tiny touch of Fall in the air. The road zigged and zagged, lending a cheerful feeling of carnival ride to her adventure. Casey's tiny truck was feeling at its best on this bright day and nothing could keep the good feelings from edging their way into Casey's heart.

She cranked up the old staticky radio and sang along to old time rock and roll at the very top of her lungs. Yep, Fall was in the air in all its long shadowed glory, and Casey was on top of the world.

She eased into the booming little town and immediately turned onto the expressway. Off on the access road and there it was. A low squat building, red brick, neatly trimmed in white. There was a middle aged man in scrubs sweeping the sidewalk and enjoying the balmy weather. "Beautiful day isn't it, Sir!" Casey chimed as she headed for the doorway. The man nodded back with a grin.

The second the door buzzed open everything changed. The smell of urine and strong disinfectant burned Casey nostrils the second she stepped in. The reception area was dark and dreary with mismatched floor tiles and shabby furniture.

Around the edges of the room sat residents in various states of consciousness. They were wheeled in and steered over to the sides of the room. Some sat in snazzy power-chairs and some in the regular hand

153

pushed ones. Some were seat-belted in so they wouldn't slide or fall. The room was dark but a fluorescent fixture burned brightly over the Nurses Station.

Casey followed the light and stood waiting for a scrub wrapped woman to finish what she was writing in a ledger. She raised a finger for Casey to hang on a second and once she finished raised her head and gave Casey a winning smile. "Hi Honey! Are you here to see one of our folks?" she asked. Casey returned the smile and kept focused on the sweet looking woman in front of her, her eyes avoiding the nasty condition of the facility around her. "Yes Ma'am. Do you have a Miss Shay living here?" A slight look of confusion crossed the woman's face but soon the smile flashed once again. "Why yes, we do. You must be meanin' Miss Dorothea Shay, right?" Casey shuffled her feet and nodded. "I'm so sorry but you threw me for a second there, Hon, Miss Shay ain't had one visitor since I can remember. You some sorta kin to her?" Casey kicked at the worn old carpet and glanced down at her sneakers. "No Ma'am, I'm no kin. I guess I'm just sort of a fan of hers is all." The woman perked right up and her glorious smile almost looked ethereal for a second. "A fan? My goodness! I had no idea we had a celebrity in our midst!" She teased. Casey returned the smile. "Oh yeah, Miss Shay was a woman of power for much of her life. I just want to get her opinion on a few things is all."

The woman reached around the tall desk and pointed down a hallway. "Her room is right down that hall there. Number 117. You enjoy your visit now!" Casey thanked the kind woman and headed down the paint chipped hallway. As she approached number 117 she had to hold on to her hands to keep from shakin' and a thin sweat broke on her upper lip. Casey stopped in the doorway and glanced into the darkened room.

Sitting near the window was a power-chair draped in blankets and afghans. The old woman turned to face Casey. "Who are you?"

Chapter 22

"Benj! Benj!" Miss Constance came barrelin' around the corner of the library as fast as her old legs could carry her. "Benj, how's Miss Casey doin' anyway? Did you get her checked for the sugar diabetes? My Lord girl, I thought you forgot all about me and all that junk spilled out on my back table. I ain't touched one thing! I been waitin' on you and Miss Casey but I've been worried into a puddle over Casey's sugar. I know how that can be Honey, it ain't a thing to mess with." Miss Constance stopped to inhale and Benj took the moment to jump right in.

"Oh, Casey's just fine Miss Constance...she doesn't suffer the sugar diabetes after all." Benj affectionately held the elderly woman's shoulder as she spoke. "Don't worry about Casey, she's just had a little spell is all." Benj tried to look as sincere as possible but just talking to Miss Constance made her smile.

"A little spell? Oh!" Miss Constance leaned in closer and whispered holding tight to Benj's arm. "Was it woman troubles? Sometimes I forget not all a us are past our time." Miss Constance knowingly nodded her head. "Well, you girls better get your little tails over't the library iffin' you're gonna take a walk down memory lane with all that ole' stuff cause I'm about to reopen next day or two and I need to get that stuff put back away. I cain't have all that smoky, stinkin' stuff sprawled out all over the table when folks are lookin' for movies to watch, now can I? Can y'all come on over tonight and take a look? Maybe after dinner?" Miss Constance looked hopefully up at Benj.

"Well, Miss Constance all I can do is ask Casey, but she might be happy to do that." Benj felt a pang of apprehension shoot through her as she remembered the last time they started rummaging. She sure didn't want a repeat of all that. "Y'all come on by. I'll be there 'til late tonight." Miss Constance said as she turned to leave.

Benj watched as the tiny little woman scurried back toward her library. She lifted a hand and waved just as she disappeared through the heavy old door.

That evening as the day was finally winding down and the western sky was splashed with blue and orange. Just as the sun was about to give up the fight for the day, Benj heard Casey's truck pull into the driveway. She stood on the porch and watched as her friend waved and unattached herself from the old pickup.

As usual Casey's arms were full of papers and charts and her scribbles of the day. She had a stethoscope dangling around her neck, three pens in her scrub pocket, with several highly suspicious latex gloves and tissues tucked into various places.

"Hey!" shouted Benj as Casey finally crawled from the truck. "How about I take you into town and buy you some dinner at the Dairy Queen tonight?" Casey stopped dead in her tracks. "For real? Can we afford that?" she asked. Benj hung her head for just a second. "Oh, probably not but let's do it anyway. Let's live dangerously and go have a damn hamburger! How 'bout it?" Casey raised her eyebrows and cocked her head. "We've got hamburger in the freezer you know, I can thaw some a that." Casey started objecting. Benj raised a hand and stopped her in her tracks. "Casey shut up! Let me take you out for once, will ya?" Casey shuffled the papers in her arms and shrugged. "I'm all for it! What's the occasion?" Benj smiled softly. "Miss Constance wants us to stop by and look at that stuff. You up for that or are you gonna keel over again?" Casey busted into laughter. "I don't think I'll keel, and that burger sure sounds like a treat! No dishes to do, no cookin'. Hell! Let's truck!"

The Dairy Queen was a poppin' place that evening as the girls enjoyed their meal. They sat on a picnic bench outside and fought the gentle breeze for claim to their napkins and papergoods. The burgers were indeed a treat along with a shared order of fries and large Dr Peppers. It seemed the whole town had the same good idea and the "Howdy!"s flew around as quickly as the burger wrappers in the soft night. Casey held the hand of one of her clients, joking with the elderly woman's son and laughing over the woman's love of soft serve ice cream.

As the crowd thinned and the dinner rush ended, Casey turned to

Benj. "Thanks for taking me out tonight. It's so nice to see these folks when you're not pokin' or proddin' them with somethin' or the next. I love this life you know. This small town world." Casey flashed a wispy smile Benj's way. "I know you do. I do as well. I'm glad we came out. I wish we could do it more often." Benj crumpled up the wrappers and two-pointed them in the nearest wastebasket. "You ready for this?" Benj softly covered Casey's hand with hers. "You scared?" she asked, looking deeply at Casey. "Sorta, but I think you're a little more scared than I am. We'd better get over there before Miss Constance takes off for the evening, huh?" Benj nodded, a look of concern crossing her face. "Yep, let's go!"

Chapter 23

As the little truck rounded the corner onto Main Street they could see the library shining like a candle in the shadowy black of the quiet streets. All of the two blocks of Main Street were bathed in darkness. The sidewalks of this town were rolled up at six in the evening and not a soul seemed to stir.

But there it was....the old library, brought into this world by the WPA during the Great Depression. The flat native stones fit together by masons with a skill long dead. The library was a grand old dinosaur of a building like many built in that era. Its imposing arches and front staircase added to its slightly dilapidated beauty. Through the large curved windows they could see Miss Constance puttering; she looked tired and beat down from this distance. Both her and the building she loved, remnants of days long gone.

"Look at her in there." Benj said. "She just loves this place." Casey patted Benj's knee. "Come on...let's get on with this."

As they entered the cool, the quiet of the stately old library surrounded them. Everything smelled dry and slightly brittle, a vast improvement over the last time they graced this doorstep. Miss Constance looked up from a pile of papers and movies she was sorting and a huge smile crossed her wrinkled face. This good woman was never without her powder and lipstick and at this late hour it all seemed just a little sadder.

"Oh girls, I'm so glad you came! I've been lookin' at that pile of burned out rubble far too long now. I need to get somethin' done with all that. Come on now...follow me." She grabbed Casey's hand as she they walked. "Oh Honey, Benj done toll me it was 'the curse' done got ya down the other day. I swear I always had such a time with that myself." Miss Constance nodded and continued to whisper.

"Sometimes I'd find myself well into a nice bottle a whisky during my 'Lady Time'." Miss Constance scurried off ahead and left Casey looking confused. "Lady Time?" she mouthed toward Benj. "Yeah, yeah I'll explain later, come on!" Benj grabbed Casey's sweatshirt and tugged her toward the back of the building where Miss Constance was flittin' around, snappin' on lights.

The overhead lamps were harsh and gave off a steady little hum that gave off a sharp crackle now and again. Casey looked up and could have sworn those were the original bulbs from back in the day...but no, they couldn't have been, could they?

"Come on in here girls let's see what we got here." The elderly woman reached into the first box.

She was tiny and slightly hunched so the reach was a big one. "Oh, my my girls, it's kinda like Christmas, ain't it? I haven't smelled this smell and touched these things since I was a girl myself." Miss Constance's face shone in the eerie light like an ethereal spotlight was glowing just above her head.

The first thing she started pulling were tarnished and battered trophies from the well packed box. She carefully and lovingly placed each one on the table in front of her. "Ya know if you take away the smoke smell it stills whiffs a my schooldays." She ran her thumb over the plaque on the first trophy. "Look at that now would ya! She exclaimed, delighted. "Earl Henry Tillman...oh, I do declare!" The old woman's eyes suddenly filled with tears "I dated Earl Henry for a little bit, ya know?" She explained, wiping her hand over her face. "He could bounce a basketball better'n anybody in school!" she sniffed.

"'Course "datin'" was a whole different thing back then. Datin' was goin' to the movies on Saturday and sittin' at the family table with ya after church, eatin' Mama's fried chicken." Miss Constance stared a long time at the Loving Cup. "Lost Earl Henry in the war just two year later. Hadn't thought of him in such a long time."

She sat the cup on the table and lovingly gave it a quick pat. Casey reached out and carefully ran her index finger over rim of the trophy. She glanced at Benj. Benj was holding tight to the edge of the table and watching Casey with all she was worth.

Casey's fingers closed lightly around one of the handles of the cup. Suddenly the dim library was gone and a handsome young face flashed in front of her. He had a big cowlick in the front of his hairline and freckles splattered across his nose. His front tooth was chipped and he was wonderfully tanned and full of life. The boy grinned at Casey and waved his hand lightly. She watched as he turned and walked up the gangplank of a ship." Miss Constance?" Casey turned toward her friend. "What, Honey? Here, take a look at this! These were the handbills for the game that was the night of the fire. I guess they were stacked somewhere and didn't burn up." Casey looked down. "Did Earl Henry have freckles?" Miss Constance looked confused. "Why, yes he did! Like an explosion across his nose!" She laughed a little. "He was cute as a button, yes he was." she stared at Casey. "Was he in the Navy?" The elderly woman smoothed the paper in front of her. "No Hon, he was in the Army. Just a regular infantry man. He was killed on a ship though...Pearl Harbor it was. Why do you ask?" Casey grabbed one of the flyers and started reading. "Oh, no reason. I just think I saw a picture of him somewhere is all." The woman chuckled softly. "You might done! He was a popular boy back then, and a hero."

With each item lined up in front of Casey, a story unfolded itself. They were brief and casual like the spot of chill left when a snowflake melts. With each item the tale of a generation opened to Casey. Some held fear and apprehension others just simple joy. These kids lived good lives; clean and happy. Most were dead now but their legacy lay in front of her in piles of ungraded papers, band medals and sports trophies.

There were few regrets in the lives of these kids though the toll it took on Casey was palpable.   "What's that?" said Benj, pointing to a small stack of papers. "Oh these were outta the office. Prolly from Miss Shay's desk. That part of the school survived better'n most. It's just an invoice for some supplies, chalk and some a those big, fat pencils. Here's one needin' more coal for the furnace signed by Mr. Buell...bless him. Here's one for some cleanin' things.

Nothin' much. That's it, girls. Well, that did bring back some memories." Miss Constance moved the box to start packin' it up again and something rattled inside. "What's in there?" asked Casey. "Oh, looks like a couple chunks a coal. Mr. Buell prolly brought it with the invoice." Miss Constance tossed the tiny chunk to Casey. Casey caught it on the fly and fell back in a dead faint.

Chapter 24

Casey woke with Benj danglin' over her with a wet paper towel and Miss Constance fannin' away at her face. The two women seemed to havin' a little spat as Casey started to gain her bearings.

"Don't you lie to me Benj! I know this girl's got the Sight! I suspected it when she dropped over before but I must say ya'll did a fine job coverin' things up!" Miss Constance was in a regular tit, fannin' and pointin' a finger at Benj.

"Hold on, hold on!" Casey pushed the two well-meaning women away and sat up. She had somehow gotten to one of the over stuffed chairs scattered willy nilly around the Library and her legs were a little stuck hangin' over the arm. "Wait a minute! Come on ladies, will ya?" she semi-shouted. " I'm all right! Stop that fannin', I'm about to catch a chill! How did I get over to this chair anyway?" Casey rubbed her hands over her face and started picking loose pieces of wet paper towel off her forehead. "Good Lordy!" She mumbled. "I carried you." confessed a downtrodden Benj. "What? You can't do that! You'll pull out somethin' in your back. I'm no little feather you know."

"Casey, Little Miss Benj over here keeps tryin' to deny you got the Sight and I'm not buyin' it one bit. I recognize all the signs! My Aunt Talulah had the Gift as well...I ain't scared a it. I wouldn't announce it over't the Pentecostal Holiness, but I ain't gonna deny it either. And I wish this child right here would stop treatin' me like I'm a pin-head idiot!" Miss Constance gave Benj the stink eye and the once over. Casey groaned and fell back in the chair. "I'm not even sure what I've got Ma'am, I really don't." Casey closed her eyes. She felt a cool dry hand touch her cheek. "Casey, I was there, I was at the school...maybe I can help."

Benj handed Casey a big cup of fresh brewed coffee. The sun was just pokin' up in the eastern sky and the day was about to be a beaut. "Why don't you stay down today. You haven't taken a day off in I don't remember when. You had a tough evening and we got home late. It's gotta be hard on you to keel over all the time, Case, who knows what it does to your body."

"I'm okay, thanks for the coffee. I'm not sure what the fallin' over does to me but you're right, it can't be terrific." Casey crossed her legs and sat Indian style propped against her pillows. "I'm tired but it'll be okay. It's box day so I'll be runnin' like crazy...that'll keep me going." Casey gratefully sipped at the wonderfully brewed cup. "When did you learn to make such good coffee? Now you're gonna have to do it more often!"

Casey swung her foot out and kicked at Benj laughing. Benj looked not only like she lost her last friend, but that friend was half dead. "Hey, get that face off you will ya? I'm fine! You look so concerned I can't stand this much attention...I'm gettin' spoiled; gonna start keelin' over at random, just for the good morning coffee...." Casey mumbled into her cup. Benj sighed. "I just wish you'd take the day and stay in bed is all. I'm going. I'm in the middle of my route.

Do what you want." Casey heard the door close and Benj's car start and back out of the driveway. She fell back exhausted into the bank of pillows behind her. It was gonna be a very long day.

By noon the idea of staying in bed was just a far off dream. Once a month, Casey went to the Senior Center and collected large boxes of basic supplies that the State provided for distribution to the elderly. Casey crammed her truck full and ran from home to home playing Santa Claus.

She would run the heavy boxes in, put the groceries away, check her folks and run out to the next. She loved these busy, happy days. Everyone loved presents and Casey loved delivering them. But this day she was tired to her bones. She had dark smudges under her eyes that even her big smile refused to hide. More than one of her clients had asked if she was okay today.

Casey leaned heavily against the cinder block wall of the Senior Center. She was there for one more box, one more delivery and the day would be hers. She closed her eyes and thought Benj was gonna have to make do with mac and cheese tonight, that's all she had energy for. As she stood musin,' she felt a heavy arm fall over her shoulders and opened her eyes to one of her favorite people. "Hey, JD! What are you doin' here?" Every day the Senior Center served lunch for those that wanted it. The food wasn't great but it was hot and nourishing. JD often said he "Wouldn't be caught dead eatin' a meal over't The Center." But here he was in all his spirited glory.

"Well, kid...I thought I'd come on over and see if I could git myself poisoned before the Good Lord saw fit to take me!" He threw back his bald head and laughed heartily. "I's in town, saw yer truck...thought I'd see what kinda trouble I could find." JD was Casey's neighbor down the highway. She stopped in and checked on him a couple times a week but he was stout man and didn't need a lot of care. JD was eighty- four years old and still climbed on his own roof to replace shingles.

"Well good to see you out and about!" Casey said, huggin' him tightly. "Well, shit-fire girl I git out more'n you do!" the old gentleman noted. Casey chuckled 'cause she knew it was the God's truth.

"Casey! Casey girl! That you over there hangin' onto that old man?" Another of Casey's favorites sidled herself across the crowded room. "Hey Miss Viola! What brings you out here today?" Casey shouted reaching out for the woman's hand. "Oh Baby, I saw you across the room and had to shout out! When you gonna come on by and make me one a them raisin pies I love so much? I sure could use a good raisin pie!" The old woman winked at Casey.

"Miss Viola you know this dastardly guy here?" Casey cocked her thumb towards JD. "A course I know him! Ain't seen him in way too ' but I know this scoundrel!" JD lifted Miss Viola's hand and smiled his damnedest. "Viola I ain't seen you since we buried my Tilda have I? An' that was over ten year ago." JD's eyes softened and Casey realized these friends had known each other since birth but hadn't had the occasion to visit.

"Come on now, you two. Why don't you sit right here and chat a bit. I'll go get y'all a cup a coffee; you can catch up." Casey wound her way through the crowd and secured two hefty cups. She glanced back and watched a few seconds as the two old folks laughed and talked and shared a wonderful lifetime in the span of a few minutes. There had been kids and grandkids and tragedy and fun.

They had lived long lives within a couple miles of one another. They knew the same people and held the same bonds. Their conversation was sweet and as easy as slippin' on an old sweater. Casey delivered their coffee, but they barely noticed she was there. As she made her way to the door for her next delivery she glanced back once again. The sort of life these two shared had a forgotten gentleness. The world was small when they were young. The only thing that separated them was war.

They knew the people in their lives for over eighty years. They had lived and worked and loved and had families all within a five mile area. Their edges were softened. They knew each other well.

Chapter 25

The staff at the nursing home had noticed a definite change in Miss Shay since the woman had visited. She was even less social and kept to herself most days. She only left her room for meals and gettin' a word outta her was a chore.

The young aide entered Miss Shay's room. "Excuse me, Miss Shay? Would you like a snack this evening? We have ice cream on the cart tonight." She said tentatively. "Get out." growled the old woman in a deep voice. "But, Miss Shay you didn't eat much of yer dinner. You sure you don't want a little somethin'? Miss Shay turned to face the youngster. "I want you to remove yourself from my room immediately and take your snack cart with you." The venom in the woman's voice coaxed the girl to turn tail without another word.

Dorothea Shay slumped down in her power-chair. She was tired and life had beat her down. She saw no reason to be cordial to these people...she saw no reason to be cordial to anyone. She would live the last days of her life just as she saw fit. She was too old to stop now. A tiny smile made it's way to the corners of her lips. She had made it to her death with her secrets intact. She no longer had to worry about anything, she was old. It didn't matter anymore what that meddlesome child poked her nose into. Dorothea Shay's days were numbered...and she was glad.

Chapter 26

Benj sat on the edge of the sofa. All the color had drained from her face as she once again read the letter between her fingers. Casey rushed in, her arms full of charts and flicked Benj's hair as she strolled through. "What's up, pup?" She shouted as she tossed her things on the bed and pulled her dirty scrub top over her head. "How was your day, kiddo? Man, I love this weather! Gonna be hotter'n Hades soon enough but for right now I'm lovin' it!"

Casey stuck her head around the corner and finally noticed Benj's state. "Hey! What's goin' on? You okay?" Benj looked up at Casey, the look of defeat spread from her head to her feet. "They are takin' my car." She announced. "What? Who's takin' your car? What the hell?" Casey plopped herself across from Benj grabbed the letter from her hand and started to read. "Oh shit."

Tears started rolling down Benj's sweet face as she watched Casey. "Case...I have to leave. I can't stay here anymore. I have to go someplace where I can make some money. I just can't live on what I make here, and there are no other jobs." Benj wiped her face and hung her head. "I love it here, Casey. This feels like home to me. I don't wanna leave but I don't have a choice."

Casey felt like a hammer had crushed her sternum. She sat quietly, barely able to draw a breath. "I figure I'll go back home for a year; one year. Then I'll get caught up with everything and come on back. It's the best I can do, Case. I can't lose my car!" Casey felt like the floor had dropped out from under her. "When are you going?" She asked taking Benj's hand. "I'll leave after the weekend. We can go have some dinner somewhere or something. Maybe treat ourselves a little before I get on the road. How do you feel about that?" Tears started the trip down Casey's face teetering on her chin and dropping to the knee of her jeans. "You know how I feel about that. Why ask?"

In the year and a half that Benj had been here Casey had once again learned to be happy with someone. She had lived alone out on this prairie in this little podunk town for years before Benj showed...she would do it again. That was all there was to it.

The day that Benj left her little farm Casey rolled home from work as usual. As she entered the house the silence draped around her like a blanket. There's something about entering an empty house that just feels different. The air is odd, the smell is just a tiny bit off. Casey walked from room to room touching things and cats as she walked. When she got to Benj's room her hand shook slightly as she turned the doorknob. The bed was stripped and the room tidy. Benj's scent lingered but the room knew she was gone, the house knew she was gone...and so did Casey.

Chapter 27

"Did you bring me my hamburger from the Dairy Queen?" Miss Ellie held the door as Casey made her way in. "No, I brought you fish." Casey raised an eyebrow and held a greasy bag out to the elderly woman. "Fish!" she exclaimed. "Well, I like fish. Where on earth did you git that around here?"

She opened the bag and stuck her nose in. "Oh my! Don't that smell good!" Casey smiled and laid out a fork and a pile of tarter sauce and ketchup. "There's some potato wedges in there as well. Sit down and eat now." Casey pulled out Miss Ellie's chair and sat down next to her. "I went over't the Quicky Mart, they have a nice fryer section now, thought you might want to give it a try." Miss Ellie spread out a napkin and laid the crispy pieces of fish out on it. "Is this a potato wedge?" She asked holding up a pipin' hot fried potato. "Yes it is...eat it! Don't wave it over yer head." Casey teased.

"Did ya hear that old man Dover, lives by the High School done walked over't the parkin' lot naked t'other day?" Casey almost spit as she poured a drink for her elderly friend. "No, I didn't hear that! Who told you that?" she laughed. "Honey this fish is a treat. I may have to send you out for this from time to time...this is good eats!" Miss Ellie smacked her lips and continued chewing. "Doris toll me." she announced. "How did Doris know?" Casey asked. Doris was Miss Ellie's best buddy and runnin' partner. Every week they packed up and took a trip to the Walmart together. "Honey, you know Doris keeps track a every naked man in this town!" With that, Miss Ellie started laughin' so hard at herself she almost choked on her fish. "Don't tell her I said that now, she'd have my skin. I like these potato wedges." Casey handed the glass of sweet tea to her friend. "Here, take a drink. Why was he runnin' around naked?" Casey asked. "He's crazy, He thinks he still teaches over't the school after all these years. That man cain't look after his self anymore. They gonna haveta do sumthin' 'bout him."

"That's the same guy used to teach out at Lawnwood right?" asked Casey sneakin' a chunk a fish and poppin' it in her mouth. "Do that agin and I'm takin' a finger!" threatened Miss Ellie. Casey laughed. "Yep, I remember back in the day he was the most handsome man I ever seen, delicate...he was a delicate man. Big, brown eyes; thin, looked a little like Rudolf Valentino only not foreign. You know what I mean?" Casey chuckled. "Yeah, it's a little racist but I get it." Miss Ellie gave Casey the Look. "It wasn't racist back then. He always looked a little sickly, but nice, clean and polished, not from around here that's fer sure, not like these homegrown farm stock." Casey drummed her fingertips on the table. "He's got dementia, huh?" Casey asked. "He's got sumthin' to be lettin' things dangle all over town! Doris wanted to go visit." the older woman laughed and swilled some more sweet tea. Casey laughed a hearty laugh right along with her. "You have a filthy mind for a Church a Christ lady, you know? I gotta scoot. Can't sit around shootin' the shit with you all day long. I got things to do. You done?" Casey pushed her chair under the table and started cleaning up. "Oh Honey, that was good. I just love when you stop over." Casey grinned. "Especially when I bring lunch!" she teased her friend. "You want me to do up these dishes before I go?" Casey asked. "No, just leave 'em. Gives me sumthin' to do this afternoon. I need to give 'em a good boil anyways." Casey nodded. She never understood why elderly folks boiled their dishes but it was one of those Okie things she was used to. "Okay, I'm outta here then." Casey headed for the door. She turned just as her friend slowly made her way to the sofa. Her legs were swollen from fifty years of being the lunch lady at the High School and standin' from dawn to dusk. Casey watched as she lowered herself into her recliner. "Call me if you need anything, will ya?" Miss Ellie waved her hand at Casey. "You know I will! Now git!"

It had been almost a year since Casey had given much thought to Lawnwood School. As she sat in her truck outside Miss Ellie's home she remembered the names and faces of the kids she'd seen the night at the Library. Sweet and cocky kids thrown into a War they didn't understand, but were willing to die for. She thought of Becky Warner and what terrible fate could have befallen her, right here in her little town so long ago. Then she thought of Benj. Casey's eyes filled with tears as she threw her truck into reverse and spit gravel haulin' outta there.

Chapter 28

Mr. Davis was a new gentleman
Casey had recently taken on. She
would meet him at the library once a
week and helped him pick out books
and movies and enjoy some time
away from his home without his
family having to worry. Casey helped
him carry things and steadied him
when he needed it. She would read
the descriptions on the movie cases
and backs of books to him. He was
alert and fun to be around. He loved
to flirt with Casey and any other
woman he happened to see. Casey
had seen photos of him in his pilot's
uniform when she visited his home

and she could understand his confidence, Joe Davis had been a very handsome boy!

"Casey! Casey!" A loud whisper made Casey's head spin lookin' for the source. She had talked to Miss Constance several times since the night with Benj, but just in passing. These whispers sounded urgent. "Casey come here a second, will ya!" Casey settled Mr. Davis into one of those comfy overstuffed chairs with a stack of books to ponder and went in search of Miss Constance. "Oh I see you got Joey Davis in yer care now. Oh my, Becky Warner had a terrible crush on him back in the day. Oh, he was tall and all muscled up back then.

He's still a fine lookin' man ain't he?"
Casey rolled her eyes. "Is this why
you've been hissin' and shoutin' out at
me? 'Cause you wanted to talk to Joe
Davis? Just come on over and talk to
the man, Miss Constance you're
eighty-three years old for God's sake!"
Casey's patience was a little shorter
these days and she regretted it
immediately.

"No, Honey I found somethin' you
might be interested in. Oh, that's not
to say I ain't gonna come over there
and strike right up with Joe any
minute, but I found a yearbook from
Lawnwood. It's the year before the
fire and I thought you might wanna
take a look." Miss Constance insisted.

She started rummaging behind her messy counter and pulled out a hard bound book. She handed it to Casey, then pulled back. "You ain't gonna keel over right here in the middle of the day when the library's full a people are ya? 'Cause if you are just come back later and git it." Miss Constance looked fearfully at Casey. "No I promise I won't keel. I haven't thought much about Lawnwood in awhile. I think some of the 'effect' has worn down." Casey explained. Miss Constance slowly handed Casey the book and waited for the worst. Nothing happened. Both women let out a sigh of relief as Casey thanked

Miss Constance and headed back toward Joe Davis.

"What's that you got there, Missy?" Mr. Davis seemed to have a hard time remembering Casey's name, so he called her any number of things that popped into his head. "Is that a Lawnwood School yearbook? Well, looky that!" He exclaimed. "I went to Lawnwood you know. Didn't graduate from there though. My family moved to Shawnee so my Daddy could get work at the new electric plant over there, so I missed my senior year. Let me take a look at that there book, my girl." Casey handed him the book and from the corner of her eye she noticed Miss

Constance circlin'. He slowly opened the yearbook, his hands just slightly shaky. Mr. Davis had been injured in the War and his reflexes weren't quite right. "Look at this, Honey! My goodness what a beautiful campus that was! All that stonework and the pond to the side...you just don't see that kinda craftsmanship these days. Schools out where I've been livin' are trailers! Can you believe that?" The old man shook his head and showed Casey the photo. Across the inside spread was a black and white photo of the school in all it's glory.

Casey felt herself slip and blackness closed around her. "Casey!" She heard and jolted back to Miss

Constance grabbin' her arm. "Sit down right here Honey and let Mr. Davis show you the book." Miss Constance guided Casey to another comfy chair and flashed her a quick "you okay?" look.

"Oh my goodness! It is my lucky day! Look who it is! Connie Buckman as I live and breathe!" Joe Davis hadn't noticed Casey's turn one bit. He had fixed eyes on Miss Constance and Casey had disappeared completely. "How you doin', Joey?" Miss Constance reached down and hugged the old man right in his seat. "I ain't seen you since you got home from the War, I swear! It's a miracle you recognize me at'all!"

Casey would swear she actually saw Miss Constance swoon! "Sit right down and help us take a look through this ole' yearbook Connie, you'd be a big help lookin' at folks." Joe Davis patted the seat next to him and Miss Constance took it.

Casey felt her phone hum and excused herself to check it. She smiled as she turned and saw the two old friends poring over their mutual, long ago, friends' photos.

"Casey, this is Donna from the office. Do you have any time on your schedule right now?" Casey closed her eyes and started counting her hours in her head. "Yeah, I might have." She said into the phone. "I'd have to sit down and really take a look though." she hedged. "Well, we have a man over there that needs help bad...and quick! Let me know when you can figure it all out, will ya?" Donna asked. "I sure will. Who is it, anyway? Anybody I know?" Casey wondered. "No, it's a new intake. His name is Dover, Stanley Dover. Over 90, some health issues but the biggest thing is dementia with him...he's gonna be 10 hours if you have the time." Casey heard papers shuffle as the news sunk in. "I'll get back to you this afternoon Donna, thanks!" Casey stood silent for a second. "Here we go again." she thought.

When Casey made her way back in the Library she took note of the two elderly people still poring over the ancient yearbook. "Oh, Casey look!" exclaimed Miss Constance as Casey got closer. Miss Constance hefted the yearbook up to face Casey "This is Becky Warner!", a beautiful blond child stared back at her. She was seated at a sewing machine and looking right into the camera. Her hair was perfectly curled and cut and she was wearing eyeshadow and lipstick. She was so achingly young and pretty Casey couldn't take her eyes off of her. "What's with the sewing machine?" Casey asked. "Oh she was Captain of the Sewing Club!

Didn't I tell you that? I guess I forgot after all these years. She could run up a dress or skirt so fast it would make yer head spin 'round. She would sew the varsity letters on all the boys jackets just as fast as they would earn 'em. " Miss Constance glanced at the photo. "She made clothes for all us girls. She was very talented." Casey continued staring at the photo. "She was beautiful. Just beautiful." said Casey.

That evening as the sun wore down and once again gave in to the fight, Casey found herself clumpin' along the quiet dirt road leading to the abandoned schoolhouse. It had been awhile since she had been out here and she wasn't even sure it was still standing...but there it was. Casey pulled her truck up the short drive and sat staring at the vacant windows, the curved steps and the neatly fit stones.

"What do you want from me, you old hulk?" She said aloud. Casey was nervous now about all this. No one had her back. No one was there if she mis-stepped. Casey closed her eyes tightly and felt a tear trickle down the side of her face. She wiped the trickle quickly. Casey knew no one was gonna save her but herself. She was all on her own and sometimes that was a hard lump for her to swallow.

She laid her head on the steering wheel and sighed deeply. As she lifted her heard she realized there was an elderly man walking toward her truck. He was dressed in overalls and a pork pie hat. He lifted a hand and smiled a warm and comfortable smile. "Evenin'!" he said. "Can I help you with somethin'?" The man laid his hand on the roof of her little truck and peered in at Casey. Casey felt a deep and wonderful warmth spread through her whole body. Y'all here for the basketball game?" The man said in a soft, mumbly Oklahoma drawl. "Well, iffin' you are, it promises to be a goodin'. Boys are in fine fettle this season." Casey looked up into the bluest eyes she had ever seen. The old man ran his fingers over his prickly face making a sandpapery sound. "Well, mind the road then. Careful 'round the corner there at the section line. The kids got a trail leadin' through there and they can pop out when yer least expectin' it. They think we don't know about it but well, we do. Don't want no dang careless kid gettin' run down." The man turned and started to walk back toward the school. Casey rubbed her eyes and opened and shut them hard. The school was shifting back and forth from the ruins Casey knew to the one she saw in the photo; full of life and grandeur. "Mr. Buell!" Casey shouted. The old man looked over his shoulder and lifted his chin. "Don't worry Casey....you're almost there."

Chapter 29

"Whoa! Mr. Davis you look beautiful!" Casey was truly impressed as she came to pick up Joe Davis for their weekly outing. He was wearing a jacket with a little bolo tie and his hair was slicked back and tidy. Casey leaned in and took a long sniff of the old man. "My goodness you smell so good! What's the occasion?" Joe Davis reached for his cane and steadied himself. "It's Old Spice. Always go for the classics, Little Girl. You can't go wrong with the tried and true. I got me a date!" Joe waggled his considerable eyebrows in Casey's direction. "A date? I thought we were going to the library today? Are you standin' me up for another woman, Mr. Davis?" Casey teased. "Yes Honey, I'm afraid I am. Though, we are off to the library, that's where my date is takin' place." Joe hobbled a few steps and turned to Casey. "Come on now Sister, I cain't be late for my first date in sixty years, now can I?" Casey held the door for him and off they went.

"So, your date is with Miss Constance, I'm gonna assume." Casey smiled as she glanced toward her passenger. "Yep, it sure is. We been talkin' on the phone like teenagers ever since last week. I declare Child, I pretty near forgot how fun it is to woo a woman!" Casey crossed her eyebrows. "Woo a woman?" She mumbled under her breath. " Yep, back in the schooldays Connie was always datin' Earl Henry, then she done married Coley Brierson, he was a no account son a sod. Please excuse my language." exclaimed Mr. Davis. Casey grinned behind her hand and agreed. "I always liked Connie but I was so taken with the wiles a that Becky Warner I never gave Connie a look-see." Joe shook his head again. "Always beware of the wiles of a fifteen year old girl Mr. Joe, they can be dangerous!" Casey teased. "They are if you're a sixteen year old boy! I was wrong not getting a good look at Connie back then though! She's a fine girl and it's better late than never, I always say!" Joe slapped his knee and grinned like a school kid. "Well, maybe in that case we should take a detour and spin by Genevieve's Flower Shop. I'm not sure a man of your distinction should show up without a flower in his hand." Casey nodded her head and looked earnestly at Joe. Joe slapped his knee so hard Casey got worried and he hooted loudly! "I do agree! We are on the same page aren't we, young Miss! To the flower shop it is!" Casey laughed and pointed her little pickup toward Main Street and the town's only flower shop.

Miss Constance was thrilled both with the flowers and the Old Spice. She immediately helped him to a nice chair at the back of the library and the two started talking and laughing, leaving Casey standing alone. She meandered over to the front desk where Miss Constance conducted business and noticed the yearbook laying to the side. Casey picked up the book and headed herself toward one of the cozy chairs. It was a rainy day and the nicest thing Casey could think about doing was curling up in this comfortable library with this book, so she did. She knew it would be a while before Mr. Davis and Miss Constance finished their "date." So why not learn a thing or two? Casey settled in, stretchin' her legs or in front of her. The only thing she needed was a nice cup a coffee, but that would have to come later.

Casey flipped through pages of Glee Clubs and school plays. The more she looked the more she realized they were just kids. Just kids growing up in a time of War. This yearbook didn't look much different then the ones she had stashed away somewhere. The town was boomin' then and the kids were clean and tidy...haircuts every Saturday. They worked hard on family farms from dawn 'til nightfall but still there they were, caught in the pages of this old yearbook. Huddled with their friends on the lovely curved steps of Lawnwood School. Leaning against the wrought iron fence flirtin' with girls, or far too shy to flirt...just watchin'. Casey smiled when she saw a photo of Eustice Buell. He was in his overalls and pork pie hat and looked a little uncomfortable gettin' his picture taken. But there he was. Old and kind, with eyes as blue as an Oklahoma sky in the Fall. Casey ran her fingertips over the yellowed pages when she found a photo of Miss Constance and Becky Warner in long skirts and bobby socks standing in the hallway. They looked like they were between classes and havin' the kind of deep conversation that only teen girls can have. She glanced at the woman this child had become. Old and bent, wrinkled and gray with the very same spark found in this ancient photo. And Becky Warner. She will always be blond and pretty. She will never be mussed or smudged. She will never have a laugh line or a wrinkle, she hadn't earned them. She didn't see her friends march off to War, never to see their little town again. Or, to come home damaged and mangled, but still children. She didn't see her town die and blow away. She didn't have to watch the peanuts wither and the cotton fields go fallow. Maybe Becky Warner had it easy after all.

Chapter 30

"Good afternoon Sir, it's a pleasure to meet you." Casey carefully took the old man's hand and shook it lightly. "Nice to meet you." he replied.

"Casey, this is Mr. Stanley Dover. Mr. Dover, this is Casey. She will be your caregiver from now on. Casey will help you do all the things you might be having a little bit a trouble with. You'll figure all that out with time but for now we'll just start with basic care." The case manager droned on with all the usual jargon Casey had heard a hundred times before. She watched Mr. Dover as the woman talked. He was indeed a fine looking man and would have been a knockout in his younger days...though he did have a "sickly" sort of pallor to him. Miss Ellie was dead on with her description. "Sort a like Rudolf Valentino without the foreign." She got it now.

The old gentleman signed papers and shook hands and smiled, though Casey had the feeling he wasn't following much of what was going on. His home was filled to brimmin' with memorablia from his days as a teacher. He had received many awards and accolades throughout his lifetime and at one time it seemed he was very proud of his accomplishments. Now, the walls of photos and plaques were covered with dust and grime. The house had a very distinct odor to it. It was the smell of neglect and dirty laundry.

When the meeting was over Casey took Mr. Dover's dry hand and looked into his watery brown eyes. "I'll be seein' you soon, Sir. It was a pleasure to meet you." The old man smiled a pretty boyish grin and nodded his head. Something in the back of Casey's mind started itching. She didn't quite get it or even know what it was, but it bothered her.

The following day when Casey returned to Mr. Dover's home the coin had flipped. He answered the door with a flourish. "Come on in, Casey...it is Casey, right? I am just horrible with names these days. I've put on a pot of coffee. Would you like a cup?" The old man walked purposefully into the kitchen chatting away as he went. "Come, come on in, Honey! Sit down, let's get to know each other a bit before we get down to the drudgery." He poured two mugs of steaming coffee and sat down across the table from Casey. He pulled two paper napkins out from under a stone frog he used as a napkin keep. His eyes were clear and a deep chocolate brown. "Don't worry, Dear. It's the disease I carry. I don't mean to scare you but I have wonderful moments of clarity and I like to take full advantage. They are few and far between. He raised an eyebrow in Casey's direction. "I woke this morning feeling just fine, I don't know how long it will last." He smiled sadly and sipped his coffee.

Casey spooned a little sugar in her cup and took a taste of the lovely dark roast. She sighed. "Mr. Dover did you teach out at Lawnwood School long, long ago? I'm sorry to just blurt that out but I've been kinda fascinated with the place." Casey sipped again. "Sweetheart, with me you have to blurt. You never know when I'm gonna disappear again. Yes, I taught out at Lawnwood; beautiful school."

He shook his head. "What a tragic occurrence." He smoothed the tablecloth with his fingertips and spooned a little creamer into his cup. "When did you start out there, Sir?" asked Casey. "Well, Dorothea and I graduated in '41 and she came straight out here. She called for me about a year later when she became Headmistress at Lawnwood." He cocked his head. "You wouldn't have a cigarette would you?" He asked slyly. "No Sir, I don't smoke." Casey replied. Mr. Dover sighed heavily and continued. "Men were going off to War right and left so Dorothea was appointed fairly fast. Of course when I came out here they wanted me to take the job just because I was a 'man' and it was a man's world back then, even more than now. I denied that favor! I still fancied myself an artist back then, all these sorry paintings and drawings around here were done by yours truly." He waved his hand around the room. Dorothea was born far more qualified than I would have ever been!" He lightly touched Casey's arm. "Mr. Dover are you talkin' about Dorothea Shay?" Casey asked, slightly confused. "Well of course, Honey. We went to Northwestern together. We were great friends back then. Dorothea has always been a bit of a wet blanket but she is as loyal as a good dog! You know I used to call her Dot just to watch her reaction, like eating a lemon! Her face would squinch up like I'd offended her honor." Casey didn't know if she should be shocked or offended. She asked the old man if he wanted a refill on his coffee and rose to get the carafe. She suddenly felt slightly dirty. "Sir, were you there when the school burned?" There was no answer. When Casey turned to the table Mr. Dover's eyes were once again dull and listless. "Mr. Dover? Do you want some more coffee?" She asked quietly. He just smiled up at her then reached out and pressed Casey's hand to his cheek.

Chapter 31

"Casey I swear to livin' God we gotta do sumthin' with this head a hair a yourn!" Miss Cheryl held Casey's head under the warm water and let the waves melt away under the stream. "I mean Honey you have beautiful hair, it's true but it's a handful ain't it?" Casey shook her head slightly. "Stop that wigglin'! I ain't gonna tolerate that. You can talk. You ain't drownin'."

Casey smiled and kept her eyes closed. A little scoldin' from Miss Cheryl always did the heart good. "I hear your over't ole' Mr. Dover's place now, huh?" Miss Cheryl asked dumping shampoo on Casey's head and scrubbin' hard. "Yep, five days a week. I have to check on him. He kinda loses track of himself from time to time." Casey explained. "Sit up Sister, git yer head outta my sink, ye'r ready to cut. I hear he's always been a little light in the loafers, iffin' you know what I mean. You seen any sign a that goin' on?" Miss Cheryl said tryin' to drag a wide comb thru Casey's hair. "Ouch! Jesus, Miss Cheryl! That's attached!" griped Casey. "Don't you be usin' the Lord's name in vain in my chair now, Sister, I'll smack you with this comb." Miss Cheryl teased. "Well, I haven't seen any Gay flags flyin' or sex toys layin' around if that's what you mean Miss Cheryl." Casey teased right back. Miss Cheryl laughed. "I don't give a hoot n' holler one way or the next, truth be known. I don't care what anybody does between their own sheets. That ain't the way everybody 'round here feels 'bout it though; sorry assed rednecks. If ye'r lucky enough to find love in yer life who the hell's bidness is it where it comes from I always say.

Jest sumthin' I heard fer years is all. What do you want me to do with this head a hair on you, girly? It's a mess!" Casey smiled. "Four inches Miss Cheryl, four inches off the bottom." Miss Cheryl humphed. "You want me to layer it some?" Casey rolled her eyes..."No!" she replied.

The day was a perfect one. A soft Oklahoma breeze was blowin' the leaves around and the sun was pokin' and ebbin' behind fat white puff clouds. Casey stopped by her last client but realized the woman had a doctor's appointment that day, so the afternoon was hers to do with what she would.

Casey ran her fingers through her new, shorter hair and checked in the rear view mirror that everything fell into place when she did. Yep, she was happy with the new haircut. Before long, the little truck started bumpin' along down the rutted road leading to Lawnwood School. Once again, it had been awhile since she had been there and she just wanted to see the place again, or that's what she told herself. Truth be known, she was hoping to see Mr. Eustice Buell.

She was so drawn to the gentle smile and kind eyes of that old dead man that she just wanted to spend time with him. She realized how odd that sounded but with all she'd learned about this old place she was really no closer to knowing anything about Becky Warner. She knew Mr. Buell suffered a terrible death lookin' for that lost child that cold, cold day the school burned. She had a good idea it was Mr. Buell that was guiding her way through the maze of War and disruption the country felt during that strange era.

Casey felt so connected to the people and events of that time. She loved the old folks. She loved the stories they told and the people they had become after leaving the wreckage of Lawnwood School. That generation was almost gone and Casey was kinda unsure of the one to follow. She loved the country those folks had formed so long ago. They had made sacrifices in their youth that had changed the course of the world, though she was pretty sure they were unaware at the time.

Casey walked slowly down the curved sidewalk holding tight to the twisted wrought iron fence. She carefully stepped up to the ornate front portico. She stepped through the doors so many children had passed before her. She could hear the whispers, she could feel the light brush of air as they walked past her. They were rushing to classes that ended decades before, but still they ran. Casey walked down the center aisle that had once held the trophy cases and doors to classrooms. She ran her fingers over the scorched stone letting her mind wander back through the ages. She glanced down the hall and saw two girls standing in long skirts and bobby socks. They were having a serious discussion...the kind only teenage girls can have.

Casey smiled widely, sadly, at the girls. A tall handsome boy came bursting out of door to the gymnasium. He was sportin' a varsity jacket and pegged blue jeans. His nose was covered top to bottom with a mass of freckles. He rushed up to the girls with a smile as big as Oklahoma itself and put his giant hands around the waist of one. She jokingly jabbed him in the ribs with her elbow.

Casey entered the first classroom. She could smell chalk dust and varnish and books. The tall windows were wide open to the bright Oklahoma sunshine and a soft breeze spun around the room lifting corners of essays and papers held down with small rocks. Even the air smelled just a little bit different, maybe just a little bit fresher; less polluted.

There was a young man teaching. He had a lovely head of dark hair that dipped rakishly down on his forehead. His soft brown eyes were earnest and full of hope. On his desk sat a stone frog holding a pile of papers that were trying hard to find themselves airborne. He had a shawl draped over his skinny shoulders and a bow tie underneath. Casey backed slowly out of the classroom almost bumping a dark clad figure wearing a long dress. The woman was young but trying hard to look much older. She had a perpetual look of sternness that could be taken as a scowl but as she glanced at the young man teaching, a secret wink passed between them. Casey watched as the woman backed out of the classroom and a delighted smile crossed her face, then disappeared as if it never happened.

Casey followed the hallway down three stairs to the furnace area. The room was badly damaged. It wasn't really a room at all anymore, just an area of stone, small and uninviting. Casey touched the stove, long gone and recycled. It was huge and round with a slotted gate at the front. Casey kicked one of the brick footings that had served for years of use and now stood cold and vacant.

She was tired, so tired. She looked up at the sky. The roof had fallen and burned, leaving the old school vulnerable to years of changing seasons. As she turned and faced the bulk of the school she saw nothing but the familiar wreckage. Through the broken windows she could see her little pickup waiting patiently for her to point it toward home. Casey slid down the stone wall and plopped to the ashes of the floor. She was so tired...her eyes closed despite her trying.

The shadows were long when Casey came to. The puff clouds had gone gray and there was the smell of rain in the air. "Oh shit!" Casey thought, jumping up as fast as her woozy head would let her. Oops! No good. Once again she slid down the stone wall grabbing the handle of the coal bin to steady herself. As she tried to stand she twisted the handle of the ancient coal bin and a shower of coal tumbled out smacking her in the shoulders. "Ouch!" she yelped, pushing big chunks of coal off of her. She sat breathing heavily trying hard to gather herself and get out of there before the rain came. Casey closed her eyes and tried to regulate her breathing. "Man! All this dream/vision crap takes it outta me!" she said to no one. Something was wrong. Casey furrowed her eyebrows and tried hard to think. She flicked a stray chunk of coal off of her jeans as she pondered. "Eustice Buell wrote out a requisition for coal the day of the fire." Casey said to herself. "I saw it myself! Then why is this coal bin so full it's tumblin' all over me?" Casey coaxed herself to stand. The sky was starting to rumble now but Casey didn't notice. She lifted the latch on the old, fire damaged coal door and pulled. A barrage of coal tumbled out to the destroyed flooring. The bin was packed full with shiny black orbs of warmth-producing coal.

Casey found a long piece of rebar and started poking in the dark bin. She used the metal to pull more and more coal to the ground around her. The sky opened up and huge splats of rain started pelting Casey's face. One more pull on the metal rod and a hand fell forward. It almost caressed Casey's face as it flopped through the open door and dangled just in front of her lips.

Casey stumbled backwards and fell hard on the ruined floor. "Jesus fuckin' Christ!" Casey screamed out loud. "Oh my Sweet Jesus!" Casey shouted. She fumbled to find her footing, but the pelting rain wasn't helping one bit. "Oh shit! Oh shit! Oh shit!" Casey screamed, trying hard to right herself. She had left her phone in the pickup and her only thought was to get there! Casey's head was swimming as she flailed in the ash and the rain. Suddenly, she felt a strong hand on her shoulder. She looked up through the pouring rain into the kindest, bluest eyes she had ever seen. She took the old man's hand and lifted herself to her feet. "Thank you Mr. Buell!" Casey shouted

above the downpour, but he was
gone.

Casey shivered and shook, running
the heat in her little truck full blast as
she waited for the police to arrive.
She didn't want to look up, she didn't
want to see the school anymore, and
she certainly didn't want to see what
was hangin' out of the coal bin. This
place had been a gentle place for her,
a haven, and now it caused only
terror. She was shakin' so hard and
didn't know how to stop. The heat
wasn't helping. The chill was coming
from inside her heart and soul.

They asked her to move her pickup when they arrived. They needed the space. Casey pulled out on the roadway and watched from there. The rain wasn't letting up and she was soaked. A kindly EMT had given her a blanket to roll up in and she did. They came all the way from Oklahoma City and set up flood lights to keep the old school lit while they searched. Everything looked so surreal to Casey in this light, and that was saying a lot coming from someone that had just walked through a day in the life, circa 1940s.

Casey watched as they brought a gurney out with a body bag laid on top of it. She closed her eyes and tears for the ages flowed down her face. The police had asked her what she was doing out here in the middle of nowhere. She was truthful and explained the ruins interested her and she came here from time to time. They had basically told her to stay put awhile in case they had more questions. She wondered now if she would feel the same way ever again about this school.

After hours of sitting, Casey drifted off to a light sleep. When she woke she knew it was deep into the night. The rain had stopped and the sky above was a blanket of brilliance.

"You can go home now, Ma'am." Casey heard from her passenger window. "What?" she replied. "You can go on home now, Miss. The sheriff says he knows you and iffin' we need anything he can call you." The young Trooper smiled slightly. "You did real good findin' them folks, Miss. Their families will be grateful." The young man nodded at her. "That was real brave a you." Casey looked confused. "What are you talkin' about Sir? Wasn't that the body of Becky Warner? She came up missin' the day this school burned down all those years ago." Casey explained. "No Ma'am. The bodies we found were all male. Young men, soldiers...prolly World War ll era. They been restin' here a long, long time." The Trooper tapped the pickup. "Go on home now. Somebody's bound to come on by and talk to ya sooner or later." He gave Casey a tired look…. "Hold on! What bodies? There were more than one?" Casey almost shouted. "Yes Ma'am. We found four so far." He tipped his hat and bounded up the embankment. Casey sat stunned. She was sure she had finally found Becky Warner. "Oh my God! Who are these guys?" She asked aloud.

Chapter 32

The second Casey opened the door she knew the house was empty. She could tell by the silence. The silence rang deep in an empty house. She found him sitting in his recliner, his head slumped to the side and a glass of Dr Pepper spilled on the floor next to him. She laid her fingers on his cold wrist and knew there was no need to hurry.

Casey's heart broke as she sat across from the old man. The Lawnwood School crowd was dwindling away. There were rumors that the school itself would be sold and demolished, Casey hoped not. She hadn't returned to the school since the bodies were found. She felt she had done her part and now she would get on with her life. She had just started getting used to her everyday routine again. She was once again starting to enjoy the company of her animals and the quiet life out on her farm. Though she had to admit things were a little less interesting since that mystery was over.

Casey often wondered what became of Becky Warner but it was a fleeting thought. It no longer consumed her like it had. Now, she sat looking at a dead man. He was old and buckled and his mind was gone but he had played a part in that long ago time. A modern day Age of Heroes. Casey picked up the phone and dialed 911. "What's your emergency?" She heard on the other end of the line. "Rena? Is that you?" Casey asked. "O' course it's me, Miss Casey, who else is gonna answer this damn phone around here? What can I do for you girl?" The friendly voice over at City Hall was one Casey knew well. "Well, I'm over't Mr. Stanley Dover's house here and I found him expired." sighed Casey. "No need to hurry, he's already taken a chill, so he's been gone awhile." Casey explained. "Oh my, girl! You need to stop findin' bodies all over the place, it's a little unsavory." The woman chuckled. "I'm sorry about Mr. Dover, but I thought it would happen a long time ago, bless his heart. He's been in a bad way for awhile ain't he." The woman said. "Yes, he has Rena. I always hate to see 'em go though it's kinda the nature of my business."

Casey tapped on the dusty counter. "Well, we'll send somebody over to collect him then. You know I think I'll just send Donnie and not bother with an emergency vehicle. You think you can hang there awhile? Save the county some cash and we know that ole' man died a natural causes!" the woman chucked. "Na, I don't mind hangin' at all. Go ahead and call Donnie." Casey agreed. Donnie was the town undertaker and a call to him would be a quiet and reverent way to get Mr. Dover where he belonged.

Casey wandered to the kitchen and did up the few dishes she found in the sink and wiped down the counters. Mr. Dover must have had a nice breakfast of toast and jam from the looks of the place. She straightened up his unmade bed and put his clothes in the laundry basket.

Casey had never been out in Mr. Dover's garage but she didn't think he would mind. It was almost empty, a few cans of dried up paint and a couple of tools. No, she didn't figure

Mr. Dover to be a tool kind of guy. The garage smelled like oil and dust and ancient grass clippings. The sun shone in through the old slats and cast dusty little beams from here to there. Dirt daubers had made nests up on the rafters, and a family of wasps were holding a serious discussion by the big folding doors.

There was an old car under a tarp smack in the middle of the old fashioned one car building and Casey's interest was piqued. She always had a love for old cars and curiosity was gettin' the better of her. That tarp had been there unmoved for many, many years that she could tell. It was the old kind, heavy cloth with grommets on the edges. Casey lifted the corner of the heavy cloth and underneath was a beautiful old Chevy convertible...dark blue with wide white wall tires.

Casey's mind traveled back to a sultry day long, long ago. A young soldier, a kid really, hitchin' back to base. A curve in the road and a dark haired young man in an open car, this open car. Casey passed out cold.

"Man, I have got to stop doin' that!" Casey said to no one as she picked herself up off the concrete floor. She brushed herself off as best she could and held tight to the wall as she made her way back in to the house. Casey dropped herself in the chair across from the dead man. "What did you do Mr. Dover? What the hell on earth did you do?" Casey asked. Finally, she picked up the phone and dialed 911 again. "Rena? It's me, Casey again. You better go ahead and send the Sheriff on out here. We may just have us a situation."

Chapter 33

Casey heard the quiet whirr of a power-chair. She watched from the corner of her eye as the black-clad figure rolled up the ramp of the funeral home. The figure rolled right up to the coffin at the front of the room and laid a flower inside. She backed the chair up right next to where Casey sat. The funeral home was empty, for all the years Stanley Dover had taught, the flip side of his life had made him a pariah.

"He was a beautiful man." the old woman mumbled. "He was a murderer." replied Casey. Miss Shay tensed noticably. "Little girl, you wouldn't understand." Miss Shay said. "What wouldn't I understand? That he was right there with John Gacy and Dean Corll? That he picked up young men and murdered them? I understand that. I don't understand the logic but I understand the action." Casey whispered. "Why are you here?" Miss Shay asked. "Because I was his caretaker and I am a decent woman." said Casey. The old woman sighed heavily. "It was a different time. That's what you wouldn't understand. He was a beautiful, creative soul. He had more life in him than anyone I have ever known. I always knew he would go places in this life, given half a chance. But, but his predisposition for young men...it was, a problem." Casey felt kicked in the teeth. "A problem? No, your water bill being late is a problem. Having your hair go the wrong direction is a problem. This was taking the lives of young men with promise and expectations. You know, there are people that have fought their whole lives so folks can love who they want. And guess what? They never killed anybody! No, Stanley Dover was a murderer, plain and simple. The old woman cringed. She turned her watery blue eyes toward Casey "He would have been strung up in this town, probably still would be. He wouldn't have been able to teach, and he was such a fine teacher." she shook her head. "He didn't kill all of them, you know. Just the ones that asked for money. He would take them to Tulsa or Shawnee and buy them a good meal. He was kind to them. He showed lonely boys some goodwill." Miss Shay hung her head. "Then he killed them?" Casey spat. "How many were there? They found fifteen different DNA profiles in that car." Casey said looking at the old woman with shock on her face. Miss Shay shrugged her shoulders. "I don't know. He asked me for help. He had a young man in the children's fort out by the schoolhouse. When he asked, I didn't know the young man was dead. After that horrible day the school burned we knew the young man would be safe in the coal. So you see Miss, I don't know how many boys Stanley "knew". I only know of the four we put in the coal."

Chapter 34

Rebecca Warner stubbed out the cigarette that had gone unsmoked between her fingers. She slowly laid the newspaper on the table next to her. The music was playing loudly but after all these years she barely heard it. A young dancer ran in, stopping abruptly next to the woman's stool. "Oh can you please fix this hem on my costume! I keep almost tripping over it and keep forgetting to ask you. I'm going on in an hour, am I too late?" The woman smiled sadly. "No Honey, just leave it on the chair. I'll get to it in plenty of time." Her hand shook slightly as she lit another cigarette. She once again turned to the newspaper. It was only by chance she had seen the article, only by chance she'd noticed it.

Everything flooded back on her like a tidal wave. Like all those years had been peeled back and the meat exposed. That one single day. The day she had slipped out of Lawnwood School to sneak a cigarette. The day the snow had come and covered everything.

Becky slipped out the gym door of the schoolhouse that day. The cold and wind immediately took her breath. She skidded around the corner and a little ways down the old path they used. Halfway down was the rough little fort the children had made years ago. In summers gone, Becky and her friends would lay on the split log floor and dream the days away. This is until Mama or Daddy caught them and put them back to work. The fort had been a haven then but was never used now. It had fallen into disrepair and the girls had gotten a bit more particular now that they were older.

Becky leaned against the wall of the outhouse and relit the cigarette she had started earlier. "Why does Miss Shay have it in for me?" She mumbled to herself. Miss Shay had called her out in class that morning making everyone turn and snicker. Becky wasn't one to hold a grudge, but today she was angry. She was so tired of Miss Shay and this school and this town; all of it. Becky had kicked at the icy ground in her anger and her foot bumped up against something. She kicked again...there in the frozen mud was a billfold. Becky flicked her cigarette off into the snow and reached down to grab the little chunk of leather. She had seen billfolds like this before, the soldiers carried them. She carefully loosened the mud and ice from the edges and flipped it open. PFC Lawrence Conway...hmmm...no one she knew.

She opened the bill compartment and gasped. The billfold was stuffed with money! Foldin' money! Becky slid down the side of the outhouse and sat on her haunches for a second. Why on earth would this billfold stuffed with money be way out here by the old fort? Becky shivered slightly. The answer to that question couldn't be good, but it was good for her. Becky's first thought was to turn the billfold in. 'Fess up about skippin' out of class and face the music.

Becky started slowly walking down the path. She passed by her childhood fort without notice. Then she started pickin' up speed. She knew town was three miles away and that it wouldn't

take her long to travel. She heard
noises behind her, shouts and excited
children... she walked faster. The
snow was fallin' at a good clip as she
made her way to Main Street. She
was cold, but excited. All around her
the town was in an uproar!
Something had happened! She
wanted to know but she didn't want
to risk it. Becky saw the big, fancy
Colliter Hotel loom out of the
whiteness in front of her. Rumbling
under the awning was a sleek and
silvery Greyhound Bus. The door was
standing open so Becky knew full well
the bus was loading. People were
shouting, "There's a fire!". Becky
crawled unnoticed onto the warm and

waiting bus. In her pocket sat her ticket outta this no account town. She ran her fingers over the smooth leather of the billfold. "Thank you Lawrence." she whispered softly. Before she knew it, the doors pulled shut and the big bus pulled away from everything Becky Warner had ever known.

As she sat starting to pull the hem out of the costume she was repairing, she realized the wallet probably belonged to one of the boys in the coal. She hung her head. Rebecca knew she had broken her family apart by runnin' off. Mama and Daddy both died soon after. Her brother went to Korea a few years later and was killed a hero. Rebecca never looked back. She glanced down at the lovely satin she was holding. She thought about the life she had lived here in the theatre. She had never been a star, but she had met a few. Maybe it wasn't the life she'd expected but it was one she had chosen. Rebecca Warner cocked her head to the music blasting on stage. She smoothed the fabric she was holding and smiled.

Lawnwood School is a real place, it actually exists...tho this is a work of fiction.

I'd like to thank Nicki Unertl for the beautiful cover photo and the day of fun exploring.

Made in the USA
Lexington, KY
24 October 2016